POPULAR REWARDS

The Enchanted Little Egg

and other stories

Award Publications Limited

With thanks to Elizabeth Dale,
Jackie Andrews, Janet Holcroft,
Jenny Jinks, Jill Atkins
and Lizzie Strong.

ISBN 978-1-78270-142-2

First published by Award Publications Limited 2017

Published by Award Publications Limited,
The Old Riding School, Welbeck,
Worksop, S80 3LR

17 1

Printed in Malaysia

Contents

The Enchanted
Little Egg

Mrs Puddle the duck lived in a quiet nest, by a quiet pond, in a quiet meadow, nestled among beautiful quiet mountains. And quiet was just the way she liked it! She went about her business in the same way every day. She would sit on her eggs, keeping them nice and warm, then she would go for a quiet midmorning swim, fly once around the meadow, and then go back to sitting on her eggs. She kept to that routine every day.

Mrs Puddle had lived on that quiet pond all her life, and her mother before that, and her mother before that, and most probably every single Puddle in history. None of them had ever left the meadow, and Mrs Puddle certainly had no interest in leaving it either. She had never met anyone other than her own family, except for the occasional migrating duck who would stop for a drink in her pond.

But she avoided them as much as she could. She had no interest in their adventures.

One evening, however, all that changed. Something disturbed the quiet night in the quiet meadow. Danger was in the air, and Mrs Puddle was worried. As night fell, she huddled a little closer around her eggs. All through the night strange noises echoed through the mountains. Smoke puffed out into the night sky, as a huge shadow swept across the meadow towards the mountains on the far side of the valley. A low, rumbling roar shook the ground, causing ripples across the pond. And then all of a sudden everything was quiet and still once more. But still Mrs Puddle couldn't sleep a wink.

By morning, Mrs Puddle was exhausted. As she went for her usual morning swim, followed by her fly round the meadow, she could barely keep her eyes open. When she flew back down to her nest her eyes closed almost before she landed! She was completely unaware that, on her quiet nest, by a quiet pond, in a quiet meadow, near a small quiet kingdom, nestled among beautiful quiet mountains, something was there that hadn't been there before. That something would change Mrs Puddle's life forever.

While she slept, Mrs Puddle had restless dreams of beasts and fire and earthquakes, and all kinds of scary things that wouldn't normally bother her. When she woke she felt very strange, and she shifted uncomfortably on her lumpy bumpy nest. Something didn't feel right.

"Perhaps one of my eggs is hatching," she thought excitedly, and she hopped off to take a look. Mrs Puddle rubbed her eyes in disbelief. She counted her eggs, and counted them again. There was definitely one more egg than there had been before.

And not only that, but the new egg was very strange indeed. Mrs Puddle waddled around the nest, looking at the new egg from every angle and nudging it with her beak. It was definitely an egg, but where had it come from? This new egg, sitting right in the middle of her nest, surrounded by her four little blue eggs, was large and purple, and twinkled and shimmered in the sunlight as though it held

some sort of magic.

It was beautiful, and Mrs Puddle couldn't stop staring at it. She looked around to see where the egg might have come from, but her nest didn't appear to have been disturbed. Not a twig was out of place; not even a footprint could be seen on Mrs Puddle's peaceful side of the pond. She checked her own eggs, but they were completely unharmed. There wasn't a scratch or a crack on them.

Mrs Puddle couldn't make feather nor tail of the whole thing, so she did something she had never done before – she took one more fly around the meadow than usual. Perhaps a migrating duck had dropped it by accident. But the meadow was just as quiet and peaceful as ever. Perhaps Mrs Puddle had been mistaken. Was it possible that she had had five eggs all along? There certainly didn't seem to be any other explanation for it. But it looked so different from her other eggs! Mrs Puddle decided that, whoever the egg belonged to, she would keep it and raise it as her own.

Nothing very eventful happened over the next few weeks, and Mrs Puddle soon forgot about the wild night, and began to prepare for the arrival of her ducklings. She even stopped noticing that she had one very strange, very beautiful egg in her nest, until finally came the day that Mrs Puddle had been waiting for.

The eggs started to wobble. One... two... three... four eggs started to crack, and one... two... three... four fluffy ducklings hatched out! The big shiny purple egg did nothing. Until suddenly... *CRACK!* A big piece of purple shell broke off, and then another, until finally, a red scaly head poked timidly out of

the top, his big, round eyes wide with wonder.

It was the strangest looking duck Mrs Puddle had ever seen! He had wings, but he wasn't fluffy, and he had a long, spiny tail. But as far as Mrs Puddle was concerned, he was just another one of her children. The little ducklings looked up at their big red brother in awe. They couldn't wait to grow up to be just like him.

Soon it was time to take the ducklings to the pond for their first swim. In they plopped, one... two... three... four... happily bobbing up and down on the water. But the fifth large red duckling wasn't so sure.

"Come on, it's fun!" his brothers and sisters called. *SPLASH!* He plopped in, spluttering and splashing, letting out a little *ROAR* as the cold water hit him.

The ducklings swam one... two... three... four... smoothly across the pond behind their mother. But the fifth duckling – large and red – splashed and struggled, letting out more little roars each time he tried to keep his head above water.

"I think we'll have to call you Rory!" Mrs Puddle laughed, as the ducklings helped Rory to stay afloat.

Next Mrs Puddle taught them to fly. One... two... three... four little ducklings leapt and hopped and flapped their little wings, but they didn't go anywhere. But Rory stretched out his long red wings and soared effortlessly up into the sky.

"Come on, it's fun!" he called to his brothers and sisters.

Mrs Puddle and her unusual family continued to grow and learn together each day, though Rory grew much bigger and faster than the others. The four little ducklings helped Rory with his swimming, teaching him to bob and paddle and dive, and Rory taught

Mrs Puddle and the four little ducklings how to soar gracefully through the skies, floating silently on the breeze and swirling through the clouds.

Life continued quietly and happily for the unusual Puddle family, until one night, when everything changed for the little family once again.

It started off just like any normal night. After their usual evening swim, they settled down in the nest: four little ducklings, with Mrs Puddle in the middle. Rory, who was already too big for the nest, curled up around them. But halfway through the night a strange sound echoed around the mountains. Rory sat up and roared quietly in reply. Gradually his roar got louder until suddenly Rory spread his wings and flew off up into the sky towards the mountains on the far side of the meadow, his roars echoing around the mountains as he went.

Mrs Puddle was in a right flap! She couldn't leave the nest, but she was worried about Rory. Where had he gone? And why? Mrs Puddle kept her eyes on the sky for the rest of the night, but by the time the sun came up Rory still hadn't returned. Mrs Puddle knew she had no choice but to try to find him. She got all of her little ducklings together.

"We're going to have to leave the meadow," she told them nervously. "We must go and look for your brother."

There were excited cheers from the ducklings and Mrs Puddle flapped them gently into formation. They were going on an adventure, and they were excited. Everyone, that is, except for Mrs Puddle. As they flew across the pond and towards the edge of the meadow Mrs Puddle started to panic, and her wings began to shake. She wasn't sure if she could fly past the hedgerows. She had never left the meadow. She had no idea what was out there, what dangers lay beyond her quiet little home. Her ducklings chattered excitedly behind her, eager to find their big brother, so Mrs Puddle took a deep breath and for the first time in her life she carried on over the edge of the meadow to the fields and hills beyond.

Mrs Puddle couldn't believe how beautiful the world was beyond her little pond in her quiet meadow, and she started to feel a flicker of something she had never felt before – excitement. She was going on an adventure, and surprisingly, it felt good!

As she neared the mountain she spotted something small and red flying around.

"Rory!" Mrs Puddle cried.

But suddenly something large swooped down towards him.

"Rory, watch out!" Mrs Puddle cried. Pushing all her fears aside, she flew full speed ahead, gliding through the air just like Rory had taught her. She had to protect him from the giant beast.

Both Rory and the huge beast disappeared into a cave in the side of the mountain. Mrs Puddle didn't hesitate, and flew straight to the cave. She landed with her ducklings just behind her, and she peered inside. All was quiet.

"Stay here," she whispered to her ducklings as she took a few steps into the gloomy cave.

Suddenly a flash of flames lit up the darkness, and Mrs Puddle could see Rory, cornered by the huge beast that Mrs Puddle now recognised as a dragon. Her mother had told her stories about the fire-breathing beasts that terrorised kingdoms, and she knew they were dangerous.

Mrs Puddle puffed up her chest and quacked bravely. "Stay away from my son!"

The dragon turned towards Mrs Puddle. Suddenly Rory jumped on top of the dragon's back, a huge grin on his face.

"Mum!" he cried. "Watch this!" Rory did a little cough, and a few little flames shot out of his nose.

Mrs Puddle stared. How had Rory done that? It took a few moments, but soon the penny dropped. And then she realised why Rory looked so different from them, why he was covered in scales and why he was no good at swimming. He wasn't a duck at all. He was a dragon! Fear welled up inside her. How could this have happened?

"Rory!" Mrs Puddle heard a shout from behind her. In flapped her ducklings, running up to their brother, who wasn't really their brother at all. "How did you do that?"

"That was so cool!"

"Teach us how to do it, please!" they chorused.

Mrs Puddle was confused and frightened. She didn't know what to do, what to think. But then the mighty great dragon spoke.

"I think I should explain," she said in a surprisingly soft and gentle voice. "When I was driven away from my home on the other side of the valley by people who thought I must be dangerous, I was scared and needed someone to look after my egg. I left it in your nest and cast a spell of dragon enchantment so you would love and care for it as if it were your own." She gave Rory a loving smile. "How can I ever thank you?"

Mrs Puddle dimly remembered that strange noisy night all those weeks ago. The next day she had found the strange new egg in her nest, but had thought nothing of it because of the dragon's spell. She could see that this dragon wasn't scary or dangerous. She was a mother, just like her.

Mrs Puddle looked sadly at Rory as he played with the ducklings, showing them how he could snort out fire, and flying loop-the-

The Enchanted Little Egg

loops round the cave. She knew she had to give him back. She was going to miss him dearly, but this was his real home after all.

"Whoa!" cried the ducklings, watching him in amazement. "I want to try, I want to try!"

Mrs Puddle knew that Rory had never really fitted in at the pond. But here he was happy; he was where he belonged, with his real mother.

And so Mrs Puddle and her ducklings returned home without Rory. But it wasn't long before they saw him again. Every week Mrs Puddle and her ducklings flew up to the mountains to visit Rory. The ducklings loved visiting their big brother and learning new flying tricks. And Rory would often visit the pond too.

The quiet nest, by a quiet pond, in a quiet meadow, nestled among beautiful quiet mountains, was never as quiet again. And that was just the way Mrs Puddle liked it.

Jasper

In the village of Heybridge there were two houses that stood side-by-side that couldn't have been more different. On one side was an old, large mansion called Heybridge House, with a long drive up to its front door. It had three storeys and a front porch held up by two stone pillars.

The house itself stood in very large grounds that were kept neat and tidy by George, the gardener and general handyman. Next to the big house, tucked to one side of the mansion's drive, was a tiny cottage. It had two downstairs rooms and two upstairs bedrooms.

Many years ago, when the cottage was first built, there was no bathroom in the house. Instead, the toilet (called a privvy in those days) was in a little hut at the end of the garden. In more recent years, though, the cottage had been brought up to date with a small kitchen and bathroom built onto the back of it. As you can imagine, this was a very welcome improvement for George and his family, who lived there.

The Hamilton-Wood family, who owned both houses, had lived in the mansion for many generations. George's family had rented the cottage for a long time, as George's father and grandfather had also been gardeners for the Hamilton-Woods.

The Hamilton-Woods' children had now grown up and left home. Mrs Hamilton-Wood (everyone called her Miss Grace) spent most of her time with her pedigree horses and dogs, which she often entered into championship shows. Her husband, James, spent most of his time in his study, working as a writer.

In George's cottage there was just George, his wife Mary, and little Angie, their daughter. Sadly, Angie had been born with an illness that meant that her legs weren't strong enough to carry her weight.

So, although doctors were trying hard to find ways to help her and make her leg stronger, she spent a lot of her time in a wheelchair. Despite this disability, however,

Angie was always very cheerful and loving. George said that he and his wife had been blessed with an angel, even if she couldn't run about and play like the other children.

One night in April, George was summoned up to Heybridge House to help Miss Grace with one of her dogs, Sandy, who was having difficulty giving birth to her puppies.

"George," said Miss Grace, feeling quite distressed, "I've rung for the vet, but it will take him a while to get here. Could you please help me with Sandy? I think one of the puppies is stuck, and if we don't help her deliver it, we might lose them all."

Although George wasn't a vet, he had helped deliver lambs and calves in the past, so he knew a bit about the process. He thought that he might be able to help, and so he set to work reassuring Sandy, who was clearly in pain and panicking. He examined her closely.

"I think the puppy is the wrong way round," George pronounced. "I'll have to try and turn him the right way."

"Oh, please do your best to help, George. It would be terrible to lose the puppies. And

Sandy is such a good mother," cried Miss Grace, with tears in her eyes.

"Don't worry, Miss Grace," George replied. "I'll do everything I can." And George did just that. After a short while, a tiny, healthy, crying puppy was finally born! George handed the puppy to its mum, who looked delighted to meet her new son, but still in some pain.

In no time at all after that, five more puppies were born. All were fine and healthy and Miss Grace looked very relieved.

"Oh thank you, thank you!" she cried, hugging George, who was very pleased but felt rather sheepish. "Maybe I won't need the vet after all."

George smiled and looked down at the six puppies cuddled up to their mum. But then he frowned, as he had noticed that Sandy herself was not looking at all well. Her head was down on the floor and she was panting heavily.

"Something's not right," said George. "I think there may be another puppy inside, and she's too tired to help it out."

"Oh no! Perhaps we should wait for the vet, George?" asked Miss Grace worriedly.

"I don't think we can, Miss," replied George. "Both Sandy and the puppy could die."

"Very well. Please do your best to save both of them; but if you have to choose, please don't let Sandy die."

George nodded, but secretly he was determined he wasn't going to lose either of them. With luck the vet would arrive before long and could take over the tricky procedure, but it was worth a shot and he had dealt with this sort of thing while delivering lambs on the nearby farms.

After some very anxious minutes, he miraculously helped deliver the last puppy, with no injury to either Sandy or the baby! Sandy looked wearily at her latest newborn and gave it a few licks to clean it up. Then she lay down and sighed, while Miss Grace stroked her head and told her how brilliant she was. George helped clean up and put down fresh newspaper for the new family.

At that point Dr Russell, the vet, arrived. He checked Sandy and each of the puppies, congratulated George on a first-class job, and gave Miss Grace some special supplements to help Sandy recover from her ordeal. Then he picked up the last puppy to be born.

"It's not surprising he had a difficult birth," he told them. "His legs are a bit deformed. You see here," he held out a tiny, crooked hind leg, "this leg is shorter than the others. He won't do too well at your championship competitions, Miss Grace!"

At this, George felt worried. He knew that Miss Grace already had many dogs, and that a lot of her time was spent making sure that they were in great shape for competing against other pedigrees! So he said to her, "Well, if you don't want to keep him, Miss Grace, me and Mary will take him on for you."

"Oh, would you really? That would be lovely," Miss Grace replied. "We will have to keep him here for a little while until he's weaned, but then he is yours to take home."

"Thank you very much," George said. "He would make a lovely little friend for Angie. They would understand each other, too, as they both have problems with their legs. What a wonderful friendship that would be!"

When George returned to the cottage it was

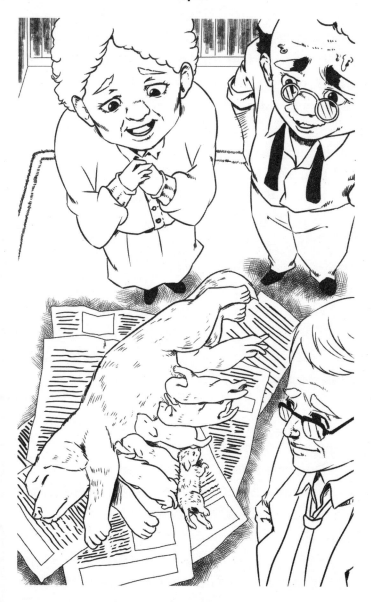

just getting light. Mary was up and preparing breakfast for the family, since she knew her husband would be hungry and tired after a long night without any sleep. Angie was already sitting in her wheelchair at the kitchen table, helping herself to the box of cereal.

"Daddy!" she cried, as George entered the kitchen. "What happened? Have the puppies been born? Is Sandy all right?"

Wearily, George pulled out a chair and sat next to Angie. Mary passed him a mug of tea, which he took gratefully.

"Well, Angie my love, it was a bit tricky. But yes, Sandy is fine. Fine, but very tired, like me! She now has a cracking new family of seven little pups."

"Oh, wow! I bet they look beautiful. Sandy is such a pretty dog; she's my favourite of them all. When can we see them?"

"Not just yet, love. We need to let Sandy have some quiet time with them, first. Then we can go up in a week or two to see them. I'll ask Miss Grace."

The days couldn't pass quickly enough for Angie. She spent the next few days trying to stay occupied. But she was too excited! She whizzed along the paths of the mansion's grounds in her wheelchair, following her father as he weeded, trimmed and tidied in the garden, all the while hoping he would take her to see the puppies.

Sometimes she wheeled herself over to the stables, to talk to the horses and give them apples and carrots, and she would visit the kennels and talk to the other dogs. All the animals liked Angie, and they were very good to her. The horses snuffled their soft noses against her face, making her laugh, and the dogs pressed up against her legs and licked her hands, as she often took small treats for them.

Meanwhile, Sandy's puppies grew fast. Sometimes Sandy would leave them for a little while and go for a brief run around the grounds. But mostly she stayed with them and nursed them as they got bigger.

Finally, one day, when the puppies had grown a little, Miss Grace and George invited Angie to meet them while Sandy was out running.

Angie was delighted and entranced, even

though she had seen a great many puppies from Miss Grace's kennels over the years.

"They are beautiful, Miss Grace!" she whispered. "Could I sit with them for a minute?"

"Of course, dear." Miss Grace carefully helped Angie out of her wheelchair so that she could sit next to the dog's bed on which the puppies were resting. Immediately they all ran over to her, jumping and licking and tugging at her cardigan with their sharp little teeth.

All of them, that is, except the smallest puppy. He struggled to keep up with his brothers and sisters, and ran with a kind of lopsided gait because of his shorter back leg. When he reached Angie, it was all he could do to climb onto her lap. Angie picked him up and cuddled him.

"This one's just like me!" she said, beaming. "Aren't you, little one?"

The little pup licked Angie's face excitedly. Miss Grace looked on and a lump formed in her throat. Two young souls had been brought together that needed special care and affection. And they were already the best of friends!

Jasper

Just then Sandy jumped back into the stall. Miss Grace was immediately afraid that Sandy might turn on Angie: new mothers were very protective of their babies. She went to help Angie up, but then Sandy came over to the little girl and flopped down beside her. Angie hugged her tightly.

"Well, it looks like you're puppy number eight!" said Miss Grace, laughing. "Wait till your dad sees you!"

"I'm going to call this little one Jasper," said Angie. "And we are going to be great friends."

Then a horrible thought struck her. "You won't sell him, will you, Miss Grace?"

"No, I won't sell him, Angie."

But in her heart, Miss Grace wondered if the puppy was going to make it. He was still a little bit poorly and weaker than the others. Sometimes the smallest in the litter didn't always survive. "In fact, your dad says Jasper will come to live with you once he doesn't need Sandy any longer."

Angie's face shone with happiness. "Oh, I'm so glad! Thank you, Miss Grace. We will look after him, I promise!"

And so the day came when Jasper came to live with George, Mary and Angie in the cottage. When the physiotherapist came to help Angie with her exercises, Jasper came along too, and Angie would rub his leg muscles for him. Sometimes he got very tired if he ran around for too long.

As the summer wore on, it was quite a common sight at Heybridge House to see Angie pushing herself around in her wheelchair while Jasper ran along beside her in his funny, lopsided way.

Watching the pair from the window, Miss Grace felt so pleased that the puppy had survived. She did often worry, though, that something might happen to Jasper, considering his short leg and that he was so weak. "I hope Jasper will be okay, you know," she commented to her husband. "He seems so small and fragile, and Angie can only do so much to protect him while she's in her wheelchair."

Her husband James looked up from his papers. "I'm surprised at you, Grace. Don't you remember your first dog, Ben? I seem to recall that he only had three legs. But he was very strong and capable."

Miss Grace laughed. "Yes he was. He was wonderful. But he seemed far stronger than Jasper!" She sighed. "Ben was wonderful."

"Well, don't underestimate Jasper," said her husband, as he went back to his work. "I'm sure he'll be just fine, and prove you completely wrong!"

It wasn't long before he did just that. One day Angie was racing round the garden path in her wheelchair, with Jasper barking and racing to catch up. Suddenly, the wheel of her chair hit a large pebble and the chair tipped up, sending Angie flying into the lake!

"Jasper! Jasper! Help!" she cried and

screamed, as she struggled to stay afloat in the water.

Without a moment to spare, Jasper plunged into the lake. He caught hold of Angie's clothes in his mouth and pulled and pulled as he paddled desperately until they both reached the side of the lake. Angie was able to pull herself out using the strength of her arms, but she was tired and panicked and couldn't drag herself over to her wheelchair. It lay overturned on the path on the other side of the lake. She sobbed quietly as she lay at the edge of the lake, feeling wet and very cold.

Despite his bad leg, Jasper heaved himself out of the water and then shook rapidly, drying the water from his thick coat. He then raced off as fast as he could to find George.

"Woof, woof, woof!" he barked at George, who was cleaning his tools in the barn.

"What's up, Jasper?" he asked. "And where's Angie?"

"Woof, woof, woof!" continued Jasper, hopping about frantically.

"Reckon something must be wrong for you to be in such a dither," said George. He threw down the shears he'd been sharpening and leapt up. "Come on then, boy. Show me!"

Jasper led George straight to where he had left Angie. She saw her dad coming and shouted, "Dad!" Though she was still very cold and wet, that didn't spoil her joy that Jasper had helped her. "Jasper got me out of the water! He's brilliant, Dad!"

George scooped up his little girl and hugged her tightly, his heart thumping with relief, trying not to think about what might have happened if Jasper had not been there.

"Come on, let's get you home and dry. We can give Jasper a treat, too."

"Woof!" went Jasper.

The story of Jasper's brilliance soon spread all round the village. People stopped by the cottage to see how Angie was doing (she had caught a chill from her dunking!), and to pat Jasper's head. They brought treats, too, for both of them.

As the days passed, the two friends spent more and more time in the gardens, sometimes just sitting side by side while Angie read a story to Jasper, or playing with Jasper's ball.

They shared picnics together, too: with dog treats for Jasper and fruit and biscuits for Angie. The pair were inseparable.

As she grew a little older, Angie's legs became stronger. Jasper had no trouble with his short leg and raced around and did all the things that energetic young dogs loved to do.

Watching the pair from her window again, Miss Grace remarked to her guest, "Those two really have a very special relationship, Janet. It's wonderful to see."

"Yes, it's really lovely," Janet replied. "I think Jasper could be trained, you know. He'd make a wonderful helper for her." Janet worked for an organisation called Dogs for Good. She trained dogs to be helpers for people with disabilities, doing all kinds of jobs that their owners couldn't manage by themselves, like picking up dropped items, emptying the washing machine and so on. It was amazing just how many things dogs could be trained to do!

"Really?" Miss Grace looked surprised. Then she had an idea. "Tell you what, Janet: if you could train up Jasper for little Angie,

I'd be happy to pay the cost. Those two really deserve the best."

Janet smiled. "I'd love to! And no charge!"

Jasper's training started shortly after – and Angie's, too, since she needed to understand how to ask Jasper to do things for her. George and Mary couldn't believe how fast the young dog learnt, or how much better Angie seemed these days.

Miss Grace had come to the cottage to visit them to see how they were getting along, and was drinking tea with George and his wife.

"Do you know, George," said Mary, "I could comfortably leave Jasper and Angie alone together. I think he would always take care of her and guard her with his life."

"You're right, love," agreed George. "It's hard to remember how that poor little puppy almost didn't make it. Just look at him now! He's a good reminder that we shouldn't ever underestimate anyone, no matter what disability they might have!"

Miss Grace blushed. "Yes, you're very right, George. One never knows what special strengths and talents other people and animal

friends have." They all looked out towards Angie, who was giggling happily with her new best friend.

Angie was pretending to drop her handkerchief and Jasper was patiently retrieving it for her and pressing it into her hand. Then she suddenly threw his ball for him, laughing. Jasper retrieved it in no time and pushed it into her hand, just like the hanky.

"Well done, Jasper," Angie cried. "I do love you! You're the best!"

"Woof, woof!" Jasper replied.

Hedgehog Rescue

"Stop it! You're scaring me! How am I ever going to get to sleep now?" Alex cried, throwing his pillow at his older brother.

James laughed, dodging the pillow as it hit the side of the tent. "You're such a baby! It's only a story. It's not real!" James giggled, passing the pillow back.

"You know I don't like ghost stories! Especially when we're out here in the dark, on our own!" Alex moaned, snuggling down further into his sleeping bag. "It's creepy enough with all the weird noises out there. I don't need you making it worse!"

Alex was always such a scaredy-cat, James thought. He had nearly chickened out of going camping, which would have really ruined it for James, as their mum had said he couldn't go on his own. What difference she thought it would make having nervous little Alex with him he didn't know, but luckily James had managed to convince him to come just in time. Just then they heard a rustling outside the tent. James and Alex froze.

"What was that?" Alex whispered.

"I don't know, maybe we should go out and see?" James whispered back excitedly, creeping towards the tent door. "After all, if I'm going to be an explorer when I'm older I need some practice!"

"No, don't!" Alex whispered urgently, trying to grab James and pull him back. "It might be a monster! Or worse!"

But James was already unzipping the tent and poking his head outside.

"What can you see?" Alex whispered nervously. "What's out there?"

"Nothing!" said James, pulling his head back inside the tent. "But it's very dark. Pass me the torch. I'm going out to have a look around. There must be something out here!"

"No!" cried Alex, "Dad told us to stay in the tent until morning!"

"Well, you can stay in here if you want, but I want to have a look!" said James, grabbing the torch and heading into the dark.

Hedgehog Rescue

Alex listened as his brother's footsteps got quieter, until he couldn't hear him any more. He started to get worried. What if something out there had got him? He thought that maybe he should go out and check. But then, what if whatever it was got him too?

Alex wished he was back in the safety of his own room, snuggled up in his own warm bed. He hated the dark. He didn't know why he'd let his brother persuade him to come out camping. It was his idea of a nightmare!

"James!" he whispered, sticking his head out into the cold night air. "James, are you still there?"

Everything was dark and quiet; he couldn't see his brother at all. Where could he have

gone? Alex crept further out of the tent, but still there was no sign of James. "James!" Alex called a bit louder into the darkness, starting to get really worried.

Suddenly an eerie glowing face jumped out at him from behind the tent.

"Woooooohhhhhh!" the scary face cried. Alex screamed and ran, tripping over the guy rope and falling headlong. He scrabbled around, trying to get up quickly, completely terrified.

Then he heard laughter, and saw James standing over him and swinging the torch around, with a big grin on his face. It had just been James all along, messing around.

"Ouch!" said Alex, rubbing his arm. "That wasn't funny, you know!" James just laughed, and went back to searching the bushes.

"Did you find anything out here?" Alex asked, sticking close behind his brother, still feeling spooked.

"Well, I think there was an owl in that tree, but I'm pretty sure your scaredy scream scared it away!" James said, still struggling to control his laughter.

They heard the rustling sound again, and James shone the torch around, looking for whatever was making the noise.

"Alex, over here!" James said. "Look!" They both peered into the bushes.

"What? It's just a prickly ball. It's probably one of Rupert's dog toys that he left under there," Alex said, looking at the round, spiky thing tucked under a bush.

"No, it's not a ball. Look closer, it's a hedgehog!" explained James. "It curled up when I shone my light on it!"

"Wow!" exclaimed Alex, "I've never seen a real one before. He's really small. Do you think he's a baby?"

"I don't know. Probably. We should leave him alone. I think we might have scared him. Let's have a look round and see what else we can see. I bet we could find some really cool creepy-crawlies at this time of night, or maybe some bats! I bet there are some vampire bats just waiting to get you..." James teased.

"Stop being mean. I'm going back to bed!" shouted Alex, running back to the tent.

Suddenly, a bright light shone on

them. "What are you two doing?" shouted an angry voice. The two boys spun around quickly.

"Sorry, Dad," James said. "We heard a rustling out here, and we just wanted to see what animals were out in our garden tonight! We found a hedgehog! Do you want to see?"

"It's very late. Just because you are on school holidays doesn't mean you can stay up all night," their dad said sternly. "You both need to go back into your tent, otherwise you will have to come back into the house. Okay?"

"Okay. Sorry, Dad," Alex said, and he rushed back into the safety of the tent. "See, I told you we shouldn't have gone out!" Alex hissed at James as they settled back into their sleeping bags.

"Yeah, but it was fun though, wasn't it?" James said, flashing him his biggest grin.

The next morning the boys woke up late after their late night. After breakfast they were supposed to pack the tent away, but James just wanted to play football.

"Come on, Alex. We can pack the tent away later!" James said, kicking the ball towards his brother. But Alex wasn't interested in playing football. "Come on, little brother, who else is going to help me with my shooting practice? I'll never be a pro footballer if I don't practise!"

"I thought you said last night you were going to be an explorer?" Alex asked, kicking the ball back to his brother. "You're always changing your mind! Last week you were going to be a chef! What next, a doctor? A clown?"

"Maybe!" James said, "Or maybe a football-playing explorer clown!" He laughed, and he kicked the ball hard to his brother. It sailed straight past Alex and into the bushes behind the tent.

"Goal!" shouted James, as he did a victory lap around the garden. Alex went to retrieve the ball from the bushes.

"James, come and look!" he called. James stopped his celebration and rushed over.

There, still curled up in a ball, was the tiny hedgehog they had seen the night before.

"Wow, what's he doing still here? I think hedgehogs are only supposed to be out at night," James said, bending down to look at it closer.

"Do you think he's okay?" Alex asked, picking up a stick to give it a poke.

"Don't poke him, you might hurt him," James said, taking the stick off his brother. "Let's get Dad, he'll know what to do."

"Dad!" Alex called, as they rushed inside. "The hedgehog is still out. Do you want to see it?"

"Hmm, that doesn't sound right. Hedgehogs are nocturnal, they should be hidden away fast asleep during the day," their dad said, following the boys out into the garden. "I'd better have a look, and make sure he's okay."

"Maybe he's hurt. Do you think Rupert might have got him?" James asked. "He might have thought he was a toy. Should we take him to the vet?"

"Hang on," said their dad as he inspected the tiny hedgehog. "He doesn't look injured. He's probably fine. I'm sure if we leave him alone he will wander off home eventually."

They put out some water and dug up some worms for it to eat, just to make sure it was all right.

"Now we need to leave it in peace, okay,

Hedgehog Rescue

boys? No more football. It'll probably be gone by this evening," their dad said.

Just before bedtime, Alex and James checked on the hedgehog. It was still in the same place, but it wasn't curled up any more. James and Alex could see its beady little eyes and cute pointy nose.

"It's so sweet!" Alex said. "Do you think we could keep it?"

"Don't be silly, it's a wild animal. You can't have it as a pet," James said. "Besides, it's not like you could pick it up and stroke it; you would get prickled!"

They noticed that the hedgehog hadn't touched the water they'd put out for it. The worms were gone, but they might have wriggled away. It seemed the hedgehog might not be well after all.

Suddenly their big, bouncy golden retriever, Rupert, bounded over to them and started sniffing around the hedgehog.

"No, Rupert, leave it alone!" James cried, trying to pull Rupert away by his collar. Rupert gave a yelp, and retreated back into the house. "Poor Rupert, I think the hedgehog might have prickled his nose!" Alex said.

"Good!" said James, "We don't want him to hurt the poor little thing!"

The hedgehog had curled itself up tight in a ball again, so the boys left it alone for the night. They hoped it would be gone by the morning. However, when Alex and James checked the hedgehog the next morning, he was still sitting there, and the little pot of water was still untouched.

"Mum, we have to do something. He hasn't had anything to eat or drink for ages. He must be really poorly!" Alex said over breakfast.

"I think perhaps we should bring him inside and put him in a box. Maybe if we keep him somewhere warm and dark, he might start feeling a bit better," their mum suggested. "If he still isn't eating this afternoon, we'll take him to the vets and see what they say."

James and Alex found an old shoe box, and put a nice cosy tea towel in the bottom. Their mum put on some gardening gloves and very carefully placed the hedgehog in the box. They put the dish of water and some more worms in there too. They put the box on the table where

Rupert wouldn't get it, and left it in peace. Alex was really worried about the poor little thing.

Later, Alex balanced the box with the hedgehog in it carefully on his lap in the car, trying to keep it steady during the bumpy journey. There had been no change, so they were taking him to the vet.

The vet inspected the hedgehog closely, and looked very worried. "It's a good job you brought this little chap in when you did. He is very poorly indeed," the vet said. "And it looks like you've done all the right things, putting him in a nice warm box, and giving him water. Well done, boys."

"We think maybe our dog might have got him," explained their mum.

"Well, there's no sign of any injury, but he is very thin and dehydrated. He wouldn't have lasted much longer out there on his own," said the vet. "The poor little thing is only about five weeks old. That means he's probably only just left his mum."

"What's going to happen to him now?" James asked.

"Well, the next twenty-four hours are critical. We'll keep him warm, and see if we can get him to eat something. Hopefully, if we can get some fluids into him, he will start feeling a bit better," she explained. "But if he doesn't start perking up soon, I'm afraid there's not much more we can do for him."

"You mean he might die?" asked James, as Alex's eyes filled with tears.

"I'm afraid it is possible," the vet said sadly. "He's so small and weak, he's got a big struggle ahead of him. But we will do whatever we can to save him. He's got a much better chance now you've brought him to us."

"I said we should have taken him to the vet earlier!" James said angrily in the car on the way home.

"Can we go back and visit him tomorrow?" Alex asked eagerly.

"Maybe we should leave it a few days, and give him a chance to recover," their mum suggested. "But if you like I will ring them in the morning to check on how he's doing."

First thing the next morning, Alex and James begged their mum to phone the vet, until finally she gave in. "Good news!" she said, smiling. "The vet says the hedgehog made it through the night, and is finally eating and drinking on his own!"

"That's amazing!" said James, giving his mum a hug.

"Can we go and see him now? Please?" Alex begged.

"Not yet. The vet said he still has a long way to go, so we can't see him yet. But in a few days I'm sure we can visit."

Alex couldn't wait to visit the little hedgehog; every day he asked his mum if they could see him. After a few days their mum agreed. They couldn't believe it when they saw how different he looked. He had bright eyes and was sniffing around at everything. He had grown a lot, too!

"Good news!" said the vet. "He's fully recovered! He's done better than any of us expected; he's a real little fighter."

"So what happens now?" asked James.

"He's ready to be released back into the wild!" the vet said, smiling.

"That's great!" said James.

Hedgehog Rescue

"Where will you release him?"

"Well, it is better for the animal if he is released near where he was found," said the vet.

"Does that mean we can take him home with us?" asked Alex excitedly.

"Well, I think the vet will have to take him," their mum said. "And he might be better in the fields behind our house rather than in our garden. It's a bit quieter there, and he'll be safe from Rupert."

"We'll bring the hedgehog round later this

afternoon, and you can watch the release if you like," said the vet. "We love getting families involved. It really helps people understand about caring for wildlife. Although clearly you already know a lot about that, as you've done such a fantastic job caring for this little one!"

Alex and James waited eagerly at home all afternoon. They couldn't wait to see the hedgehog be released back to his home. Alex stared out of the window, watching every car go by, hoping it was the vet. Eventually the vet pulled up outside and got out with a little animal carrier. "They're here!" Alex shouted, running to get his mum as the doorbell rang.

They took the hedgehog round the back of the house to the big field.

"This is a great home for a hedgehog. Nice and quiet with lots of hedgerows. He'll be very happy here!" the vet said, as she placed the box carefully on the grass. "Everyone be very quiet and still, and we'll see what he does."

She put on some gloves, carefully took the hedgehog out of the box and placed it on the grass near a hedge. The hedgehog just sat there for quite some time.

Hedgehog Rescue

"Come on, little one!" whispered Alex, willing the tiny creature to run off happily. Eventually the hedgehog took a few steps towards the hedge, and then scurried off to find his home.

"That was so cool!" breathed James.

"Thank you so much for looking after that little hedgehog," the vet said to James and Alex. "You really did save his life."

Later, over dinner, James and Alex were telling their dad excitedly about their fun day releasing the hedgehog back into the wild.

"Maybe we should go out into the garden later and have a look," suggested their dad. "He might still be somewhere nearby. If we go out after dark we might catch a glimpse of him."

When it finally got dark, Alex, James and their dad went out into the moonlit garden. This time Alex wasn't the least bit scared of the dark. He was excited. He couldn't wait to see what interesting creatures they would see. Hopefully they would see their friend, the hedgehog! They stood still in the darkness and listened hard. They heard all sorts of noises.

Some bats flapped around over their house and an owl hooted somewhere close by, but there was no sign of the hedgehog.

"Well, we can't stay out here all night," their dad said after a while. "Let's go back in. It's getting late."

"But we haven't seen the hedgehog yet!" Alex protested.

"We might not," said James, disappointed. "He might have moved on somewhere else. He could be anywhere by now."

They started to head back into the house, when Alex suddenly heard a rustling. "Wait, Dad, I can hear something over here!" he whispered, creeping towards one of the bushes. His dad and brother looked around, shining the torch on the bushes.

There, poking its little nose out from under some leaves, was the tiny hedgehog. He sniffed around for a few seconds, stopped and looked at them, and then scurried back under the cover of the leaves.

"I think he came out to thank us!" Alex said, excitedly. "Bye, little hedgehog!"

"Well, let's hope that's the last we see of

him," said James, as they headed back inside.

"But why? Don't you like him?" asked Alex, confused.

"No, I really liked him," said James. "But if we don't see him again then hopefully it means he is happy and healthy."

"Only thanks to you two boys!" said their dad. "I'm very proud of you both."

"You know what," James said, looking back around the garden, "I think I'm going to be a vet when I'm older!"

Alex and his dad laughed. "You mean a football-playing explorer clown vet?" Alex teased.

"Maybe!" said James, laughing.

The Scaredy-Cat

Fluffy was a farm cat – a very pampered farm cat. She did very little during the day, spending most of her time relaxing on the rug in front of the nice warm fire, drinking cream from her favourite china bowl, or having her long, fluffy grey coat stroked by the farmer's wife.

One evening, however, while Fluffy was lying in her favourite spot, stretching her long fluffy legs after a lovely warm snooze, she overheard Farmer McMurray talking to his wife.

"I just don't know what we're going to do," Mrs McMurray said. "It's a real problem."

"It's eating the corn, scaring the lambs and chewing holes in the feed. Something has to be done about this mouse!"

Mouse! Fluffy froze in fear. She was not the bravest of cats. In fact, she was definitely a big old scaredy-cat. And if there was one thing that Fluffy was scared of more than anything else, it was mice. Which was rather unusual for a cat!

"There's only one thing we can do. Fluffy will have to go out and get rid of it," Farmer McMurray said.

Fluffy's ears pricked up. Go out? Surely not. Fluffy never went outside if she could help it. It was cold and dirty out there. She quickly hopped up and rubbed her back against Mrs McMurray's legs, purring loudly. Mrs McMurray was a softy. She always gave Fluffy extra treats off her plate at dinner and pampered her as much as she could. There was no way she would ever send Fluffy outside.

"I suppose you're right. It is the only option," Mrs McMurray said, leaning down and stroking Fluffy's back. Fluffy flinched, and tried to run for it, but Farmer McMurray scooped her up and carried her to the door.

"Out you go! It's time you earned your keep," he said as he gently pushed Fluffy outside. "No more sitting in front of the fire all day. Once that mouse is gone you can come back in."

Popular Rewards

The Scaredy-Cat

And with that Farmer McMurray slammed the door shut, leaving Fluffy outside in the cold, dark, wet and windy night. Fluffy curled up, her eyes wide with fear as she listened to the strange noises of the outside world. Every creak and groan of a tree branch or howl of the wind made Fluffy shiver. The hooting of an owl made her fur stand on end, and she spent the night shivering and shaking, curled up against the barn door. She didn't get a wink of sleep.

When the sun finally came up, Farmer McMurray opened the front door and Fluffy made a dash for it, grateful to finally be let inside. She had done her job and kept mice away for the night, and it was time to get back to her usual spot by the nice warm fire. Unfortunately, Farmer McMurray had other ideas.

"Oh no you don't! You need to come with me," Farmer McMurray said, picking Fluffy up and carrying her down to the barn. "Now get to work. You're a cat. Scare some mice!"

Meanwhile, in the barn, hiding among the hay bales, Mouse froze. He had heard the word 'cat' and he was scared. Mouse lived a quiet life on the farm. He slept in the nice warm hay, ate the yummy corn that the farmer brought in from the fields, and loved playing with the baby lambs. Everything had been perfect, until now.

Mouse peered around the edge of one of the hay bales and gasped as he spotted Fluffy. She was sitting there on the straw in front of the bags of corn, looking big and fierce, with long sharp claws, big pointy teeth, and a grumpy face. A shiver went down Mouse's spine. If there was one thing Mouse knew, it was that cats liked to chase and eat mice!

Mouse's stomach gave a loud rumble, and he shot quickly back to the safety of his little hole in the hay. He was hungry and he needed to get to the corn. But he couldn't get there without passing right underneath the cat's nose. Mouse's tummy rumbled again. There was nothing for it. He would have to be brave.

Mouse spent a while watching Fluffy. She didn't really do much, Mouse thought, and she certainly didn't seem to be searching for mice like the farmer had said. She curled up on the straw, flicking her tail back and forth, flinching at every sound, and looking very miserable indeed.

When Mrs McMurray brought Fluffy out a dish of cream for her lunch, Mouse's tummy growled even louder. The cream looked good. Mouse knew that now, while the cat was distracted, might be his only chance to get to the corn. Slowly and carefully he crept out of his hole and lowered himself down to the barn floor. He tiptoed as quiet as, well, a mouse!

As Mouse crept past the bowl, Fluffy froze. She could tell that something was there without even looking up from her bowl.

Mouse froze as Fluffy's face slowly emerged from the bowl. First came her big black eyes,

then her shiny black nose, long wiry whiskers and big sharp-toothed mouth…

Mouse squeezed his eyes tightly shut as Fluffy opened her mouth wide, showing off all her shiny, pointy teeth…

"AARGH!" Fluffy cried.

"AAARGH!" Mouse squeaked.

"Don't hurt me!" they both cried together.

"What?" said Mouse, totally confused. He wasn't being eaten! Instead, the big scary cat was cowering away from him.

"S–stay away," Fluffy stuttered, slowly backing away from Mouse into the corn bags behind her. Suddenly Fluffy didn't look nearly so fierce and scary after all.

Mouse paused. If he didn't know better he would say the cat was scared of him. But cats aren't scared of mice, are they? Perhaps it was a trap. Mouse looked around, poised and ready to run, but nothing happened. And Fluffy still looked terrified.

Mouse pulled himself up big and tall, puffed out his cheeks, and squeaked his loudest fiercest SQUEEEEEAAAAAAK!

"Miaaaooow!" Fluffy cried, jumping up and

landing on top of one of the bags of corn.

Mouse tried his hardest not to laugh at the funny sight before him. Who had ever heard of a cat being scared of a mouse? Perhaps he could use this to his advantage.

"Let me have some cream, and I'll leave you alone," Mouse said as loud as he could, whilst trying very hard to hide the fact that his knees were knocking together in fear.

"Okay," Fluffy said quickly. "You can have some. But please don't hurt me."

Mouse moved slowly towards the bowl of cream, keeping an eye on Fluffy the whole time, still not entirely trusting her. Quickly and hungrily he lapped up some of the delicious creamy drink. Now what?

"Now, I'd like to eat some of the corn in that sack," Mouse said, nodding at the sack that Fluffy was sitting on.

"You can't," Fluffy said, suddenly remembering why she was out there in the first place. If she let Mouse continue to eat the corn, then she would never be allowed back inside the nice warm house. Fluffy thought of her comfy rug by the fire, and she shivered.

All she wanted was to be back in her home, being fussed over and stroked by Mrs McMurray, eating up the leftovers from her plate. It was Wednesday, which meant they would be having macaroni cheese tonight, Fluffy's favourite. Suddenly Fluffy had an idea: one which would hopefully make sure the mouse wouldn't hurt her, and would also get her back inside the house. "I–I can't let you eat the corn, but I can get you some cheese…"

Mouse's eyes lit up. Cheese was Mouse's favourite thing in the world. He almost never got to have any. He only ever managed to have a taste when the farmer dropped some from his lunchtime sandwich. And even then he had to be quick to beat the pigeons.

"How?" Mouse asked, narrowing his eyes suspiciously.

"I'll get it for you. But there's something you have to do for me first," Fluffy said, and she quickly explained her plan to Mouse. Mouse wasn't sure at first. Could he really trust a cat? But when he looked at Fluffy, her hair still standing on end with fear, he knew that she wasn't really a threat. If she had wanted to eat him she would have done it by now. And this way, they both got exactly what they wanted. It was a win-win situation.

"You've got yourself a deal," Mouse said, and they both smiled.

Fluffy waited until she heard Farmer McMurray's footsteps coming towards the barn as he finished his final jobs for the evening. Suddenly she felt a CHOMP. Something small had bitten her long fluffy tail!

"MIAAAAAOOOOWWWW!" Fluffy cried, looking around at Mouse as he squeaked with laughter, running out of the barn at full speed.

Fluffy chased after Mouse, hot on his heels, as Mouse squeaked with fright trying to get away. But Fluffy was faster. She pounced and landed right on top of Mouse, catching him in her paws. Mouse wriggled and squirmed, trying to get away. Fluffy looked up to see Farmer McMurray watching her expectantly, so Fluffy opened her lips wide and picked him up in her mouth. Mouse squeaked loudly in protest.

"Good girl," Farmer McMurray said, giving Fluffy a stroke. "I knew you could do it. There'll be an extra treat for you tonight. Come on, then. Let's go home and have tea."

Fluffy smiled, which was surprisingly hard with a mouth full of mouse, and trotted along ahead of Farmer McMurray, eager to get back to her comfy spot in front of the fire.

Once she was safely back inside and Farmer McMurray was in the kitchen eating his dinner, Fluffy opened her mouth wide and spat out a very bedraggled Mouse, who was curled up in a ball and dripping wet.

"Yuck!" Mouse groaned, shaking himself dry.

"Yuck? I'll never get the taste of mouse out of my mouth now. And did you have to bite my tail so hard?" Fluffy cried grumpily, licking her fur to get rid of the disgusting taste.

"Did you have to eat me?" Mouse asked, unhappily.

"As a matter of fact, yes," said Fluffy. "And it worked, didn't it? The farmer needed to know I had got rid of you, otherwise neither of us would be getting any dinner." And with that her tummy rumbled loudly. She had barely eaten all day and she was starving.

The Scaredy-Cat

"You'd better hide. They'll be back in soon."

Mouse tucked himself under the edge of the rug just as Mrs McMurray brought in a large plate of macaroni cheese and placed it in front of Fluffy.

"What a good girl, getting rid of that mouse," she said, giving Fluffy a stroke. Fluffy purred happily, glad to be back where she belonged. She kept one eye on the corner of the rug where Mouse was hiding.

When Mrs McMurray was gone, Fluffy sniffed the plate longingly. She could easily

gobble it all up herself, but she had made a promise. Fluffy pushed the plate over to where Mouse was hiding, and, possibly for the first time in history, a mouse and a cat shared a meal together.

"I suppose I had better go," Mouse said once they had licked the plate clean. He looked out at the howling wind and rain. "Unless... perhaps I could stay?"

Mouse still wasn't sure he could trust cats. After all, he had spent quite long enough inside the mouth of one today! But he didn't want to go back outside either. He quite liked the comfy rug by the warm fire, and Fluffy seemed quite friendly after all.

Fluffy thought hard. She still wasn't sure she could trust mice. After all, Mouse had bitten her tail very hard earlier. But she knew that if Mouse went back outside then she would just get sent back out to catch him again. And Mouse didn't seem too bad, for a mouse. This way they both got exactly what they wanted.

"You've got yourself a deal," Fluffy said, and they both smiled.

The Scaredy-Cat

And probably for the first time ever, a cat and a mouse settled down together on the rug in front of the nice warm fire and fell fast asleep.

The Little
Lost Bunny

It was a beautiful sunny afternoon. Isabella was having such fun playing with her friend Carly and her new puppy in her garden.

"Fetch, Basil!" she cried, throwing a ball and watching the eager puppy bound off after it. The little spaniel was delighted to be playing the game and ran back to them eagerly with the ball in his mouth. He dropped the ball at Carly's feet and lay down on his back so that Carly could rub his tummy.

Isabella loved the puppy. She thought he was so cute and sweet and she loved playing with him. She wanted so badly to stay and play, but soon her mum would be here to collect her and take her home. Isabella longed for a pet of her own, but no matter how much she begged, her parents always said no. They told her that she wasn't old enough to look after it, that she'd grow bored, and that they would be the ones left caring for it. But she knew that they were wrong. If she had a pet of her own she would look after it and love it more than anything. But how could she prove it, if they wouldn't even give her a chance?

There was a knock at the door and Isabella heard Carly's mum talking to hers. She ran inside to meet her and give her a hug hello. The little dog trotted in happily behind her and sat patiently at her feet, with the ball still in his mouth.

"Hi, Mum! Look at Carly's new puppy!" Isabella said to her. "Isn't he adorable? And he's so well behaved!"

"Oh, yes. He's very cute," her mum said, bending down and stroking Basil affectionately. "Right, come on then, Isabella. Time to go home." Isabella frowned at her mum's lack of interest.

On the way home Isabella thought she would have another try at persuading her mum. "Please could we get a pet, Mum?" she pleaded. "I would look after it really well, I promise!"

Her mum sighed. "We've talked about

this before, Isabella. Dogs are a lot of work. Owning one is a big responsibility." Isabella felt disappointed, her happy mood vanishing rapidly.

At dinner, Isabella pushed the last of her food around on her plate thoughtfully. "You know, it wouldn't have to be a dog," she said. "If we got a guinea pig it could eat up all of our leftover vegetables. Or a hamster! Err... I mean, we could get a hamster – not that the guinea pig would eat one!" She giggled. "A hamster wouldn't take up much space at all!"

But to her dismay her parents still said no.

That night, as her mum tucked Isabella into bed, she brought up the subject yet again.

"Carly takes her puppy for a walk to the park every day," she said. "She gets lots of healthy exercise. If we got a dog, we could take it for walks together and get exercise too."

"Not this again, Isabella," her mum said. "Carly's mum is home all day to care for their puppy. But your dad and I work all day while you're at school, so no one will be here for it. Anyway, how do you expect to look after a pet if you can't even keep your own room tidy?"

The Little Lost Bunny

Isabella looked at the mess around her bedroom and realised that her mum had a point. And so she decided she was going to make some changes. She would prove to her parents she was responsible enough to look after herself, and therefore responsible enough to have a pet!

Over the next few weeks Isabella worked really hard. She kept her room very tidy, helped her mum around the house, and did her homework without being asked. And she didn't mention a pet once. Her parents were very pleased with her good behaviour!

One day on the way home from school, Isabella saw a worn, cuddly blue toy rabbit lying abandoned on the pavement. She picked it up.

"Look, Mum, someone must have dropped this. They might be looking for it. What should we do?" she asked.

Isabella's mum stroked the soft fur, brushing off some leaves and twigs. "We'll leave it here on top of this fence and hopefully whoever lost it will walk back and find it," she said.

But the next day, the rabbit was still there. "Mum! Look, the bunny is still here. No one has claimed it," she cried. "Please can we take it home?"

"It's old and dirty, darling!" said her mum.

"Please? I will clean it up, I'm sure I can make it all nice again!"

"Oh, well, okay," said her mum, looking unsure. "If you really want it that much."

Isabella happily picked it up and when she got home, she ran straight upstairs and gave the bunny a warm soapy bath, carefully washing all the dirt off it. Then she gently rubbed it dry with a towel, and brushed its fur until it looked as good as new. She then set to work on a very important task. A short while later she ran downstairs for dinner, carrying some sheets of paper. She held one up to show her parents.

"I thought we could put these up along the route to school. That way maybe we can find its owner." In her hands was a poster with a beautiful big drawing of the cuddly blue bunny.

Underneath the picture the words 'FOUND

– one very lovely bunny wanting to go home' were written in big letters. She had also written their phone number in her very best handwriting.

"Whoever has lost this bunny is probably very sad, and it would be so lovely if we could return it!" Isabella said eagerly. "Can we go and put them up now, please?"

"That's a very lovely thought. And you've put so much work into those posters. Well done, love," said her dad, smiling proudly. "No one will be out now, so you can put them up in the morning."

The next day on the way to school Isabella and her mum put all of her posters up. When she came home she asked if anyone had

phoned yet, but no one had. So Isabella took the bunny to bed that night and cuddled it tightly, just to keep it safe. By the following morning there had still been no phone calls. Isabella began to think no one would ever claim the bunny.

"Don't worry, Bunny, I will look after you," she whispered lovingly to it. She gave the bunny a quick squeeze, and secretly slipped it into her school bag. She played with Bunny that day at lunchtime, and she realised that she was really growing to love her new friend.

However, when Mum picked her up from school, she had some news for Isabella.

"Good news! Someone has phoned about the bunny!" she told her. "They said their little boy dropped it on their way to the shops, and that they had been looking for it everywhere! They were so pleased when they saw your poster. They're coming round in half an hour to pick it up."

"Oh," frowned Isabella. "That's good."

"Aren't you happy?" her mum asked her, looking at her closely. "You've managed to help reunite the bunny with his owner."

"Yes, it's wonderful news!" said Isabella, although she didn't feel quite as happy about it as she was trying to sound.

When the family came to collect the bunny later that afternoon, they brought some rabbit-shaped biscuits as a thank-you. The little boy's face broke into a huge smile when he saw his cuddly bunny.

"We're so relieved to have Nibbles back! Ben has been so sad without him, he hasn't been able to sleep," said his dad. "And look how lovely and clean Nibbles is! You have obviously looked after him really well. Thank you so much," he said to Isabella, smiling warmly.

Isabella handed the bunny over and watched as the little boy hugged it so tightly, gurgling with joy. She was still a little bit sad that the bunny had to go, but she saw how happy it made him, so she knew that she was doing the right thing.

Isabella was unusually quiet over dinner that evening, and her parents watched her as she silently went upstairs to get ready for bed without being asked.

The Little Lost Bunny

The next day after school both of Isabella's parents were there to pick her up, with big smiles on their faces. "We have a surprise for you," Dad said as they walked home.

When they got back they went straight out to the back garden. Sitting there, with an enormous pink bow wrapped around it, was a hutch. And inside, just poking its little nose out, was the most gorgeous, tiny, black-and-white rabbit that Isabella had ever seen. She stared at it in amazement.

"It's gorgeous! Is it really for me?" she asked in disbelief.

"Yes, it's for you," said her mum. "You have been so responsible lately, keeping everywhere tidy and working hard."

"And we were so proud of what you did for that little boy and his toy bunny," added Dad. "So we thought perhaps it was time we rewarded you with something that you really want."

Isabella smiled so much her face ached. She gave her mum and dad a huge hug, and knelt down in front of the hutch. Eagerly, she got her new rabbit out for a cuddle, snuggled into its soft warm fur, and sighed with happiness.

"Thank you so much!" she said. "This is the best surprise ever."

"So, what are you going to call it?" asked Mum.

Isabella knew straight away without having to think. "I think I'll call it... Nibbles!" she said. They all laughed together.

The Wickedest Witch

Once there was a young girl called Willow. She was no ordinary girl: she was a witch! Willow went to a boarding school called Enchanted Towers, the top magic school for witches in the country. This might sound very exciting, but actually Willow hated school. Enchanted Towers was one of the oldest magic schools in the world. It was very traditional, and witches were taught how to be the worst type of witch – a wicked witch! But Willow didn't like being wicked. She much preferred spelling to spells; she enjoyed cooking more than making potions, and she wanted to use magic for good, not evil! She knew that if the other witches tried, they would prefer being good too.

She had wanted to go to a normal school and not use her magic at all, and she pleaded with her parents to let her change schools. Eventually, they had let her try a non-magic school. And for a few days it had been great! She loved having normal lessons, and playing with ordinary children. But she hadn't yet learnt to control her magic, and strange things kept happening when she was around.

The other children started to avoid her, and whispered about her behind her back. Eventually, after a few too many unexplained incidents, she was asked to leave. Everyone was relieved that she was gone, but Willow wasn't. It meant she would have to go back to Enchanted Towers!

The school wasn't the only place where witches weren't welcome. Everyone believed that all witches were wicked, and wherever they went people avoided them. Willow hated that. But with places like Enchanted Towers producing more and more bad witches, it wasn't really surprising! So Willow was stuck going to that horrible dark castle day after day, being taught how to do all of the awful things that gave witches a bad name.

As if all of that wasn't bad enough, at the end of every year at Enchanted Towers they had a special prize ceremony. And the one prize that everyone really wanted was 'Wickedest Witch'. Everyone except Willow, that is. This meant that for weeks beforehand, all of the witches tried out their meanest tricks, spells, potions and curses on each other, to show off just how wicked they were. It was awful. You never knew when the next spell was going to hit, whether your lunch would turn you green, or your book might try to bite you. Willow hated this time of year at Enchanted Towers even more than the rest of it.

That time of year had come round again. The sounds of crashes and bangs, screams and cackles rang throughout the school, as every witch tried desperately to win the contest. The smell in the school was awful as cauldrons bubbled with brewing potions filled with disgusting ingredients like toad's legs and fly's wings. The very thought made Willow's skin crawl, and the smell made her stomach churn.

Willow didn't want to enter the competition. She had no interest in being wicked. However, not competing was not an option. If the teachers thought you weren't trying, you got detention, or worse! The year before, Willow had decided she definitely wasn't going to take part, and had done as many good things as she could instead. As punishment for breaking the school rules, she had to let some of the first year students practise their spells on her every lunchtime for a week.

Every part of Willow had turned a different colour. She had had green toes and purple fingers, an orange face, and blue legs. And worst of all, her hair turned into snakes for two days until someone could find a spell to change it back! They kept trying to bite her, and no one would go near her! It had been the worst week of her life. So this year Willow knew she would have to take part, one way or another. There was no way she was going to risk going through that again. "We haven't seen any wicked spells from you yet, Willow," said Miss Grimspell one afternoon during wand-work. Miss Grimspell was probably the worst of all the teachers at Enchanted Towers.

"I've got something great up my sleeve, don't worry!" Willow fibbed, hoping Miss Grimspell wouldn't ask any more questions.

"We need to see some effort from you soon,

The Wickedest Witch

or there will be consequences! Remember last year," Miss Grimspell said, glaring at Willow over her glasses.

Willow shuddered at the memory and patted her hair down. She could almost feel it slithering around again. Willow knew she would have to think of something, and fast, to keep the teachers satisfied. As Willow walked along the corridor to her next potions class, she saw a big pot already bubbling away ready for them. It was a thick and purple, so Willow knew it must be a vanishing potion.

Suddenly, Willow had a great idea. If she made the potion spill on the floor, everything in the classroom would disappear. They wouldn't be able to have the lesson if there was nothing there! It would be great! It wouldn't hurt anyone, and it would look like she was trying to be wicked, so it might save her from detention a little longer. Willow grabbed her wand from the pocket of her cloak and muttered the spell under her breath. The cauldron started to wobble.

Unfortunately the headteacher, Mrs Battle, was standing next to the cauldron just as it toppled, and the potion poured out over the floor, splashing her legs! Everyone stopped and stared as Mrs Battle's legs began to disappear. Then gradually more and more of her vanished.

Mrs Battle didn't notice what was happening until only her head and shoulders were left. A look of surprise crossed her face, and then it quickly changed to anger, as finally the last bit of her head disappeared, and she was gone! It was as if she had never been standing there at all! There was complete silence for a few seconds as all the witches tried to take in what had just happened. Then suddenly everyone let out a huge cheer.

"Who is responsible for this?" came Mrs

Battle's angry voice. Everyone fell silent immediately. They had forgotten that, although they couldn't see her, she was, in fact, still there. Everyone looked around for the culprit. Willow, aghast at what she had done, was still standing there, wand in hand, frozen in fear.

"Willow Skylark!" Mrs Battle's voice thundered. "Everyone back to your classes. Willow, I will see you in my office this evening after dinner."

Everyone scurried away quickly, whispering and giggling about what had happened. Willow just stood there, still shocked by what she had done, and terrified about what Mrs Battle would do.

By the end of the day, everyone had heard about what Willow had done to Mrs Battle. It was all anyone could talk about. Everywhere Willow went people were congratulating her, as if she had already won the wickedest witch competition.

"I can't believe you did that. You're so brave!" said one witch.

"I wish I'd thought of that. You're going to

win for sure!" said another. They all looked at her admiringly. They wouldn't be so keen when she got her punishment, Willow thought. She tried to explain that she hadn't meant it to happen, but no one would listen.

Willow sat miserably at dinner, trying not to think about what was awaiting her in the head's office in a few minutes' time. One witch, who Willow recognised as the student responsible for her snake hair the previous year, sat down next to her. "What you did was wicked!" the girl said, looking at her in awe.

"What?" Willow snapped. She wasn't really in the mood for small talk, especially about her stupid trick.

"Sorry. I was just saying your trick was wicked! Really cool! You must really want to win the competition!"

"Wicked?" Willow said thoughtfully. "Yes, I suppose it was, wasn't it?" An idea formed in her head. Perhaps there was a way for her to win the competition after all! If only she could convince everyone else to think the same way that she did… Suddenly she wanted to go to the head teacher's office. She hoped she would listen. As soon as dinner was finished, Willow made her way up to Mrs Battle's office, and knocked on the door. "Come in," came Mrs Battle's voice.

Willow walked into the room. But she couldn't see Mrs Battle. She was still invisible! This was going to be even more awful than she thought, talking to an empty room! Willow sat down at the desk and started talking.

"I'm sorry, Mrs Battle. This wasn't supposed to happen," Willow explained. "I didn't want to enter the competition in the first place! Miss Grimspell said I would get detention if I didn't compete, but now I'm going to get detention anyway, or worse probably."

"Miss Skylark," Mrs Battle said. "I am over here!" Her brisk voice was coming from somewhere behind Willow. Willow spun around and saw her standing by the door. She was back to normal! That was something, at least."I'm so sorry, I thought you were... I mean, I thought you weren't... I mean..." Willow didn't quite know what to say.

"Willow, stop," Mrs Battle said. "I've thought long and hard about this, and I have decided that I'm not going to punish you."

Willow stared at Mrs Battle in shock. "What? But why not? I should be punished. I made you invisible!"

Mrs Battle stared at Willow over the top of her glasses. "Do you want to be punished?"

"Well, no, of course not. But I probably deserve it," Willow explained. This was not going how Willow had expected at all.

"But you were only doing what had been asked of you, and it was an accident. Therefore, I can't very well punish you for it," Mrs Battle said. "As I would like to," she added.

"But don't you see how backwards that is? You can't punish me for doing something awful, because you always want us to be awful! I don't understand why a school would want to encourage its students to be wicked. We're special. We should use our magic for good!"

Mrs Battle's stern expression softened into a much kinder one. She sat down on the other side of the desk and sighed. Willow felt very nervous as she waited to hear Mrs Battle's response. Finally, she broke the silence.

"You remind me a lot of myself when I was

your age," Mrs Battle said, with a sad look in her eyes. "I always thought it was a shame that witches were told they had to be wicked."

Willow stared in shock, not sure whether to say anything or not. She couldn't believe Mrs Battle was saying this.

"The problem we have is this," began Mrs Battle. "We are witches, and witches are wicked. It is expected of us. This school has a tradition of producing the most talented, most wicked witches there are. Think of every story you know about witches. There's never a wonderful witch, is there? Being wicked is what we are supposed to do!"

"But why can't we change that?" Willow asked. "We can prove the stories wrong! We can't be the only ones who want to be good!"

"I don't know how..." sighed Mrs Battle, putting her head in her hands. "People will always be scared of witches. It's just the way it is, and I wouldn't know how to begin to change that, no matter how much I might want to."

"Well, I have an idea how to start," Willow said. She couldn't believe that stern Mrs Battle, who everyone was afraid of, actually wanted to be good too! She started to wonder how many of her classmates hated being wicked as well. She finally felt hopeful that it might be possible to change things.

When Willow finally got back to her dormitory, everyone rushed to talk to her. "We thought you had been expelled, you were in there so long!" Winnie said.

"You must have been in so much trouble. What punishment have you got, cauldron cleaning?" Esmerelda, another witch, asked.

"Oh, it's not that bad. But I am tired. I think I'll just go to bed," Willow said, as she headed upstairs with a smile. Behind her she heard the other girls still speculating about what had happened in the head teacher's office. Willow thought about everything that had happened that night. She'd done all she could to convince Mrs Battle to do the right thing. Now she could only hope and wait.

Finally, the last week of term arrived, and with it the prize-giving ceremony. All the witches were very excited as they gathered in the courtyard. Everyone chatted amongst themselves, discussing who they thought might win. Willow heard her name mentioned a few times, and felt people staring at her, but she tried to ignore them.

Willow was more nervous than excited. She'd waited her whole life for a day like today, and she could only hope that she had inspired Mrs Battle enough to go through with her idea. And now the time was finally here, she worried about what all the other witches would think. After all, this was a very traditional school, and one that hadn't, in the past, been good with change

Mrs Battle finally took to the stage. Willow couldn't be sure, but it looked as though Mrs Battle was shaking. She looked as nervous as everyone else, and she certainly wasn't her usual stern, imposing self.

"Time for the prizes!" she announced. Everyone clapped and then fell silent, hoping to hear their name called out. There were prizes for each subject first, and everyone cheered and clapped the winners. When it came to the final prize of the day, the much anticipated Wickedest Witch title, everyone held their breath.

The Wickedest Witch

"I'm sure you all know what the final prize is," announced Mrs Battle. "However, I've decided it's time for a change."

Everyone looked round at each other, wondering what was going on.

"It's time to stop being stuck in the past," Mrs Battle continued. "It's time we all realised that witches don't have to be wicked!"

Everyone gasped. They couldn't believe there was going to be a change. It was unheard of! Enchanted Towers had been run the same way for centuries, encouraging bad behaviour in witches. Even the other teachers looked shocked.

"So," continued Mrs Battle, "there will still be a prize for the Wickedest Witch. But this year, the 'wickedest' will now mean the 'coolest'. And we have one witch here who came up with the most wicked, brilliant plan to change this school, and hopefully our lives, forever. Willow Skylark!"

Willow almost fainted in surprise.

"This brave young lady questioned what it is to be a witch. She wanted more from life than being nasty and scary, and being feared by everyone. And she was right. I hope you all agree, and will embrace the changes we are going to make." Silence echoed around the courtyard, and Willow didn't know whether to go up on the stage, or run away and hide!

Slowly, some of the witches and teachers began to clap, until finally almost all of the crowd were cheering for her. Willow went up to collect her certificate, and people were congratulating her and cheering her name as she went. Willow felt amazing. She couldn't believe so many of the witches agreed with her idea!

Over the next few years at school there were many changes. Miss Grimspell resigned. She couldn't see why any witch would want to be nice, and didn't want to have any part in it! But all the other teachers and pupils loved the changes. Subjects switched so that pupils were using their magic for good, rather than evil. Witches were given marks for being kind and friendly, rather than mischievous. Extra points were awarded for charity. Dark magic was completely banned.

Willow finally started to love going to school.

The Wickedest Witch

At last she was learning how to do the good, helpful magic that she had always wanted to do. She knew it would take a long time before non-magic people weren't afraid of her any more, but they had taken a step in the right direction.

All the students at Enchanted Towers still competed hard to get the wickedest witch prize, but they no longer did nasty spells and horrid potions. Instead they had to do fun and helpful incantations. They were so proud to be recognised for their good work, more than they ever had for being nasty. Many years later, Willow became the head teacher of Enchanted Towers, and continued to run it just the way she wanted to: with fun, and excitement, and lots of good magic. The 'Wickedest Witch' prize remained the highest award you could receive. She also decided to rewrite the stories about witches. She wrote lots of books about kind, funny, and helpful witches. Gradually things got better between witches and non-magic people.

And one day, Willow decided to write the story about her adventures at her awful school, and how, with the help of her head teacher, she changed the meaning of 'wicked witch' for all witches everywhere!

The Tale of Pipkin's Tail

Pipkin Pony lived on a farm with his mum and all his brothers and sisters. But while Polly, Peter, Pegasus, Petal and Penny had beautiful long tails like their mum, Pipkin had a short, stumpy one!

"Neigh!" whinnied all the brothers and sisters as they wrinkled their noses with laughter. "What a silly tail!"

Pipkin didn't like being laughed at. So when his brothers and sisters went out to gallop in the field, he stayed with his mum. He put his head under her long, warm neck and snuggled up to her.

"My brothers and sisters are laughing at me because of my tail," he complained.

"Take no notice," said Mum. "You're lovely just the way you are. Why don't you go out and play?"

"They won't play with me. They think I'm

different and so they don't like me. I wish I had a long tail like you and my brothers and sisters," he said. "How can I make mine long?"

Mum sighed. "Why don't you go and ask Claris?" she suggested gently. "She might know."

Pipkin peeped outside. His brothers and sisters were rolling in a patch of mud in the middle of the farmyard. They turned their backs on him as he trotted by.

"We don't want to play with you!" they whinnied unkindly.

He looked at their long tails and blinked hard. He didn't want them to see him cry. It would give them something else to tease him about. Instead, he found Claris Cow. She was in the milking parlour. Claris peered up at him with her big brown eyes.

"Hello, Pipkin," she mooed.

Pipkin's legs trembled, but he plucked up the courage to speak.

"Hello, Claris," he said. "Can I ask you something, please?"

"Of course you can," mooed Claris. "What do you want to know?"

"I wondered if you could tell me how I can make my tail long?" asked Pipkin.

Claris leant forward and took a good look at Pipkin's tail.

"Moo!" she mooed. "If I were you, I'd eat plenty of grass. That might do the trick."

Pipkin was happy with this idea, but felt that it was a little unusual as he and his family already ate plenty of grass and it hadn't helped him so far. But he thought it was worth a go, and so he trotted round to the back of the milking parlour and out onto a quiet field on the farm. He found some fresh grass and ate and ate until he was full to bursting. Then he hurried to the water trough to look at his reflection.

Popular Rewards

But whichever way he twisted and turned, his tail was still the same.

"Oh!" he sighed. "It's not long yet."

A few spots of rain landed on his nose as he made his way back to the barn. Mum Pony nickered gently as he lay down beside her.

"How did you get on?" she asked.

"Claris Cow told me to eat grass, but that didn't work," said Pipkin, turning round in front of Mum. "Look, my tail is still short."

"Oh dear," sighed Mum. "Never mind."

"But I do mind," said Pipkin, feeling a tear trickle down his nose.

Mum wiped away his tear. "Why don't you go and ask Hector? He might know."

So Pipkin trotted across the farmyard in the rain. He passed his brothers and sisters, who were whinnying and snorting. Luckily, they were too busy grazing to notice him.

He knew where to find Hector Horse. He was always in his own barn at this time of day. The big wooden doors creaked loudly as Pipkin pushed them open and went in. He stood well away from Hector. Hector wasn't so different from him, but as a horse he was bigger than a pony and had massive hooves. Hector blew down his nose and nodded his big head. Pipkin took a deep breath and opened his mouth to speak.

"Hector," he began, "do you mind if I ask you something?"

"Of course I don't mind," whinnied Hector. "What do you want to know?"

"I wondered if you could tell me how I can make my tail long, like yours?" asked Pipkin. Hector stared down at Pipkin's tail then nodded his head.

"See that spring on the door over there?" he neighed.

Pipkin looked at the big coiled spring on the barn door and nodded.

"Why don't you wrap your tail around that, and try pulling? It might make the hairs longer," snorted Hector.

Pipkin went to the door and carefully wrapped his tail around the spring. The rain pattered heavily down. Pipkin stayed there for a long time in the rain. He grew wetter and wetter. Eventually, he unwrapped his tail and trotted to the pond. He looked at his reflection, but whichever way he twisted and turned, his tail was as short as ever.

"Oh no!" he sighed again. "It's still not long!"

On his way back to the barn, he watched his brothers and sisters for a moment. They were galloping about and ignoring him as usual. He trotted past them into the barn and sat down beside Mum Pony.

"Did that work?" she asked.

Pipkin shook his head and curled up beside her again, trying to get warm.

"No," he said. "Hector Horse told me to pull at my tail to make it stretch, but it's still as short as ever."

"Oh dear!" nickered Mum Pony. "But you know... it doesn't really matter."

"But it does matter!" sighed Pipkin. "I want to be like the others."

"Oh dear," said Mum Pony. "Why don't you go and ask Sheppy? She might know."

"All right," said Pipkin. And so he made his way to the shed at the side of the farmhouse, where Sheppy the Sheep Dog was having a bath. When she saw Pipkin, she jumped out of the bath and shook herself. Pipkin jumped back as water sprayed all over him.

"Sheppy," he whinnied. "Do you mind if I ask you a question?"

"Of course I don't mind," barked Sheppy. "What do you want to know?"

"How I can make my tail long?"

"Woof!" Sheppy barked as she sniffed Pipkin's tail. "See how long my hair is after my bath? The water weighs it down. Dip your tail in the water here. That might do the trick."

Pipkin dipped his tail in the bath of warm soapy water. It felt lovely and comforting and Pipkin was sure it would do him good. After a while, he left Sheppy and trotted to the pond for the third time to look at his reflection, but, as before, whichever way he twisted and turned, his tail had not changed at all.

"Oh no!" he sighed. "It's never going to be long!"

Sadly, Pipkin trotted past his brothers and sisters. They were still having fun, but the rain was making the field very wet and muddy. It didn't look like fun to him! Pipkin went into the barn and sat down in front of Mum Pony.

"Any good?" she asked him.

Pipkin was too sad to answer. He went into a corner and buried his nose in a pile of straw.

"I wish you would believe me," said Mum Pony. "You're lovely just the way you are!"

At that moment, Pipkin heard loud, distressed neighing from the farmyard.

"Help! Help!"

It sounded like one of his brothers and sisters. What was the matter? Pipkin jumped up and went to the door of the barn. He was amazed at what he saw. The rain had stopped and Penny was stuck in some oozy, gluey mud and couldn't get out! Mum Pony came to stand beside him and see what the matter was.

"Oh dear, what silly ponies they are!" she neighed.

Suddenly, Pipkin had an idea. He felt very brave. His legs felt very strong.

"Hang on!" he whinnied as he dashed across the farmyard. "I'm coming!"

When he reached his sister, he turned round so that she could see his tail. None of his brothers or sisters were laughing at him now.

"Hang on to this," he whinnied. "I'll have

you out of there in a jiffy."

Penny latched on to her brother's tail with her mouth. He pulled and pulled and pulled. Slowly she was able to move enough to pull herself out of the mud. They all cheered when he finally pulled her free.

"Pipkin rescued me!" whinnied Penny.

"She held on to his short, strong tail," said Pegasus.

"He pulled Penny out," announced Peter.

Then they all turned to Pipkin. "We're sorry we laughed at you, Pipkin," they whinnied together. "You're wonderful just the way you are!"

"And don't you ever forget it, Pipkin!" said Mum.

Pipkin felt warm and tingly all over as he snuggled down with his muddy brothers and sisters. And from that day on, they never teased him again!

The Guinea Pigs' Holiday

Bramble and Rose were two guinea pigs that lived with their owner Ellie and her parents. They had a nice warm house in the shade of an apple tree, and at night-time and when the weather was bad, Bramble and Rose slept there.

Outside in the garden they had a very large run which they could play in. Ellie was good at keeping their house clean and giving them lots of fresh hay and green vegetables, and her dad helped her move their run once the guinea pigs had eaten all the grass. They had a very nice life!

But, like so many people who have everything they need, Bramble and Rose began to get bored. So, when Ellie came to bring them their breakfast one morning and told them she was going on holiday in a few weeks

The Guinea Pigs' Holiday

with her mum and dad, it gave Rose an idea.

"Why don't we take a holiday, too?"

They were both lazing sleepily in a warm patch of sunshine on the lawn, munching on the tasty, crunchy food pellets that Ellie had given them.

"What do you mean?" asked Bramble.

"Well, I know that when Ellie goes on her holiday, we'll probably go to that place where they look after us while she's away. What is it called?"

"Pigs 'n' Buns," said Bramble, scornfully.

"It's a little home for guinea pigs and rabbits. Don't you remember?"

"Oh, yes. It is all right here, I suppose, but what if we went away on our own instead for once? Somewhere nice."

Bramble rolled over and sat up. "Where would we go? And how would we get there?"

Rose absently picked a grass stalk and chewed it while she thought. "It wouldn't have to be far, as we'd have to walk and carry our things with us."

"I suppose we could go camping in the wood that Ellie talks about. The one with the stream running through it."

"Oh, yes! Sleeping under the stars, foraging for tasty leaves, listening to the birds…"

"Paddling in the stream…"

The pair went quiet, each lost in a daydream, travelling on their perfect imaginary trip. They had little smiles on their faces. Then they got up and skipped excitedly round the lawn. "Yes!" they squeaked. "We'll do it!"

Over the next few days, Bramble carefully saved portions of their food and hid them under their house, where Ellie couldn't see them. Because of this, their food always seemed to disappear so quickly! Ellie gave them a little bit more than usual, as they seemed to be extra hungry.

Rose worked on making a hole in the wire of their run. She had found a corner where it had lifted from the frame, and by working at it and gnawing at it, managed to make it big enough for them to squeeze through.

As soon as they were ready, the pair crept out late one afternoon, each clutching their food parcels wrapped up in large cabbage leaves. Out of the run they went, and under the garden gate. And that's when they met their first problem.

"Which way, Rose?" whispered Bramble. Neither of them had any idea where Ellie's wood might be.

Rose stared around. Ellie's house was on a modern housing estate. There were plenty of roads, but not too many trees or green places. There certainly wasn't a wood in sight.

"Er..."

Before Rose could answer, there was a deafening roar as a car swept past them, spewing out nasty fumes. The two guinea pigs squeaked in alarm and dived for cover behind a large bin, which had been put out for the recycling lorry to collect. Trembling, the pair stayed hidden, convinced some terrible monster was after them.

"Wh–what was that?" whispered Rose, once the noise had gone.

"I don't know, Rose. But we can't stay here. Besides, this bin smells horrible."

"Yes, you're right. I can just see some green stuff over there, look! Maybe that's where the wood is. We'll have to cross this hard ground first."

"On three, then," said Bramble. "One… two… three!"

Running as fast as their little legs could go and clutching their cabbage bags as they went, the two guinea pigs scampered across the road, across the pavement on the other side, and quickly disappeared into a jungle of weeds. And, as they discovered, a load of rubbish!

"Eww! This isn't much fun," remarked Bramble, as he pushed his way through all the overgrown weeds on the wasteland. There were plenty of old bottles, tins and crumpled food wrappers, too.

They were a short way into the jungle when Rose gave a shriek. "Bramble! Look out!"

A large tabby cat had been watching them make their slow progress. His tail was twitching, his eyes large and round, as he made ready to pounce. But when Bramble stood up on his hind legs and shrieked at him, the cat put back his ears, hissed and jumped, then ran off, deciding to leave the strange new creatures alone.

"Oh, Bramble. That was very brave. That cat looked horribly fierce."

"We've seen cats before, Rose," he reminded her. "They often come into the garden. You

just have to do the unexpected. If we had run away, it would have chased us. Come on, let's see if we can get out of this horrid place – and mind where you put your feet."

The evening was still light, but it was getting late. The guinea pigs needed to find somewhere to shelter for the night, and both of them were feeling rather peckish.

"Do you think we could stop for a moment and have a bite to eat?" Rose asked.

"I suppose so. But we mustn't eat everything. We need to save some for our holiday."

As they pulled some food out of their little bags, Rose was thinking that holidays weren't quite as easy as she had imagined. She hadn't thought about cars or wastelands. Or cats, come to that!

They each ate a few pellets and carrot pieces and then refolded their cabbage bags. No sooner had they done that than a large, round, black-and-white missile landed right by them with a loud *THUMP*. It was followed by the shouts of children and the thunder of running feet.

"Quick, Rose! Hide!" urged Bramble. They ran and hid underneath a crumpled piece of newspaper.

Four children were playing football and making a lot of noise. One lad picked up the ball from where it had landed near the guinea pigs and ran back to his friends, shouting as he went, to continue their game.

Bramble peeked out from under the paper. "It's clear again, Rose. You can come out now."

But Rose didn't come out. In her nervousness she had chewed some of her cabbage bag and, since the contents had fallen out, decided to eat the rest. She felt miserable.

"Oh, Bramble. This isn't the holiday I imagined. It's much too dangerous. And we'll never find the wood. I can't help thinking of our nice house, and the garden, and Ellie. I wish we'd never left."

Bramble kissed her nose tenderly. "Don't worry, Rose. It'll get better, you'll see. Would you like a piece of apple?"

Rose sniffed and wiped her nose with a paw. "Thank you, but I'm rather full. I'm afraid I just ate all my rations."

"Ah," said Bramble, thoughtfully. "Well, we can just share mine."

"Thanks, Bramble, but I honestly think we should go back home."

Suddenly they heard some loud barking. A dog had joined the children in their football game! If the ball came their way again, the dog would be bound to chase after it and would maybe discover the two little holidaymakers!

Feeling very alarmed, Bramble said, "Perhaps you're right, Rose." Cats he thought he could deal with, but dogs – especially large ones – were much more terrifying! He dropped his cabbage bag. "Come on, let's get out of here before the dog finds us."

They turned to scoot back the way they'd come, but the sun had disappeared behind some clouds and it was not so easy to see any more. The guinea pigs relied on their noses and sense of smell to find their way back to the road, and neither of them were looking forward to crossing it again.

To make matters worse, it started to rain. Heavily.

"Oh, no!" cried Rose. "This is too much!

The Guinea Pigs' Holiday

Bramble, we'll never manage to get home!"

They paused on the edge of the rough grass, rain dripping off their tiny noses, feeling utterly hopeless.

"There they are!" a familiar voice cried out. "Dad! Mum! I've found them!"

It was Ellie! She was running towards them, looking left and right to check that there were no cars coming, followed closely by her parents. She was overjoyed at finding her guinea pigs safe, and she swept them up into her arms. "Bramble! Rose! Where on earth did you go? I was so worried!"

Once back home, the two guinea pigs were given a gentle rub down with a warm, fluffy towel, and put back into their hutch with fresh nibbles and treats. Ellie's dad had already mended the hole in their run.

"Well, Rose…" Bramble began, as they both relaxed once more in deep hay.

"No, don't say it, Bramble," said Rose. "From now on we'll take our holidays at Pigs 'n' Buns!"

Felix and the
Friendly Fairies

Felix was a little pixie who lived with his mother. Although he was only little, he was very well behaved. And he loved his mother dearly. He always tried to be kind, and would help her with the chores whenever he could.

Each night at bedtime, Felix's mother would tell him wonderful stories. Felix loved listening to them and believed that they were all true.

One day, Felix's mother fell ill.

"Can I go and fetch you some medicine, Mother?" asked Felix.

"No, dearie," replied his mother. "It's just a cold. It'll be gone in a week."

But it was not just a cold, and it certainly did not go away in a week's time. The truth was that Felix's mother did not have any money to buy medicine. Her illness became worse and worse, until she couldn't even get out of bed.

Felix was very sad. One afternoon, a friend of his, Kip, came to pay him a visit.

"What's the matter, Felix?" asked Kip. "You look so glum!"

"My mother is very ill," said poor Felix. "And we don't have enough money for medicine to make her well again."

"That's terrible," said Kip. "Let's try to think of something that we can do to make her better."

"I'd love to," said Felix, gloomily. "But I can't think of anything that might help her."

"Think harder, Felix," said Kip. "You're always so full of wonderful ideas. If you can't help, can you think of anyone who could?"

Felix thought hard. Suddenly, he jumped up in excitement. "I know who can help!" he said. "The Friendly Fairies!"

"Who are they?" asked Kip. "Do they live around here?"

"No," said Felix. "No – the Friendly Fairies live far, far away. Nobody knows where, exactly. But they would certainly be able to help Mother. I'm sure of it!"

"That's great, Felix," said Kip. "But if nobody knows where they live, how will we find them?"

"Hmm," said Felix, scratching his head. "I'm not sure about that. But I can't leave Mother and go and look for them, and she is too sick to come along too."

"What if we could send the fairies a message?" asked Kip. "That way, they can cure your mother from wherever they are."

"Kip, you're brilliant!" said Felix. "I'm going to find a way to send them a message!"

Felix ran back home to tell his mother about

the idea and to think up a plan. His mother smiled weakly. "Oh, Felix," she said. "It's very sweet of you to be worried about me. But the Friendly Fairies are not real, they're just make-believe. It's all right, though. I'll be better soon."

"I'm sure they're real, Mother," Felix insisted. "And I'm going to ask them to make you better."

The next day, a determined little Felix made his way to the post office. The postman knew almost everyone's address, but even he didn't know where the Friendly Fairies lived.

Felix didn't lose hope. He sat with Kip and thought hard: "How do I send someone a message if I don't know where they live?"

"Well, I think you should write it where they cannot miss it, no matter how far away they are."

"Kip, you're a genius!" said Felix once again. "I know just the right place – the moon! Everyone in the world looks at the moon at night. I'm sure the Friendly Fairies will see my message if I write it on the moon."

"All right," said Kip, stroking his chin. "But

who will go to the moon for you?"

"A cow, of course!" said Felix. "Haven't you heard the nursery rhyme? Cows are known to jump over the moon. I'm sure they would also be willing to leave a note there on my behalf."

"Oh!" said Kip. "Well, it's worth a try. We can borrow my father's cow."

That night, the two friends coaxed Kip's father's beautiful cow, Bessie, out of her barn. Felix had made a large banner for the Friendly Fairies to see. He rolled it up and tied it to the cow's collar.

"She's ready to go!" he said.

"Go on, Bessie! Jump!" instructed Kip, but Bessie simply stayed still and continued to chew.

"Perhaps we should startle her a little," suggested Felix. He tugged Bessie's tail gently, but she whipped it out of his hands and kicked towards him in annoyance. She accidentally tripped Felix over and he fell flat on his back in the the mud!

Kip yelled in surprise and looked down at Felix.

"Oh no! Are you okay, Felix?"

"Yes, I'm fine thank you, Kip. I'm not hurt," Felix replied. He stood up, brushing the mud off himself as he stepped away from the cow. "This clearly isn't working. I'm so disappointed! What am I going to do? I can't let my mother stay unwell. I have to find a way to help her get better."

Kip shrugged. He could see that Felix was getting very frustrated that his plan wasn't working. "We will work something out, Felix," said Kip. "Don't worry. Go home to your mother. We'll try again tomorrow."

When Felix had gone home, Kip got to work. He untied the banner from Bessie's collar and re-wrote the message onto a small piece of paper, copying Felix's handwriting as carefully as he could. He then made his way to the home of Comet, the astronomer.

Comet was an old astronomer who mostly kept to himself. Nobody in the village ever really saw him as he didn't ever come out or socialise with anybody. He wasn't unkind, but he liked to keep himself to himself. He lived on his own in a tall tower on top of the tallest hill. At the top of his tower, he kept a huge telescope through which he watched the stars, the moon and planets every single night.

Kip knocked on the astronomer's door nervously. When it opened, a serious-looking man with a long beard appeared, dressed in beautiful robes covered with stars and planets. "Yes?" he said in a deep voice.

"Er, hello. My name is Kip," said Kip, feeling a little scared. "I've come to ask you if you would be so kind as to help me with something."

"That depends," replied the astronomer. "What kind of help do you need?"

"I can explain it to you in detail if I would be allowed to come into your home?" Kip said, feeling even more nervous.

"All right," said the astronomer. "I'm quite curious. Come in."

Kip told Comet all about Felix's wish to put a message on the moon for the Friendly Fairies, and explained his plan to help Felix and his mother.

"I know it is a lot to ask, but I was wondering if you could help us? Felix's mother really is very sick."

Felix and the Friendly Fairies

To Kip's surprise, Comet readily agreed to help him. They discussed the plan for a few minutes, and then it was time for Kip to go.

"Thank you, Comet," said Kip, as he got up to leave. "You've been very kind and generous. Felix will be thrilled!"

The astronomer smiled. "From what you have told me, Felix sounds like a lovely fellow. I would like to help him. Let's hope that the plan works. Goodbye!"

By the time Kip got home, he was smiling and feeling very happy. Both Felix and his mother were going to be just fine!

The next day, Kip ran over to Felix's house to give him the good news. "Felix, guess what?" he said. "Last night, after you left, I managed to get Bessie to jump over the moon. She dropped your banner there, just as I told her to."

Felix was overjoyed to hear this. "Oh, Kip, you are such a good friend!" he cried. "I can't wait for tonight, when the moon comes out. The Friendly Fairies will be able to read my message, and Mother will be well and fully healthy again!"

"Let's go to the astronomer's tower and ask if you can use his biggest telescope," said Kip. "Then you will have a clear view of your message on the moon."

That evening, before it got too dark, the two friends made their way to Comet's tower. Kip pretended to be meeting him for the first time.

"Hello," he said. "We're sorry for bothering you. My name is Kip, and this is my friend Felix. We hope it's okay to turn up on your doorstep like this. But may we use your telescope, please? Felix has sent a message up to the moon, and it's a rather important message. He would like to see it and was hoping you could help him."

"Hello there! Of course, of course," said Comet. "Come right inside. I'll set up the telescope for you." And with that, he went upstairs.

"He's surprisingly friendly," whispered Felix. "I thought he liked to keep himself to himself."

"No, no," said Kip. "It's probably because he's asleep during the day that we don't see him in the village."

Felix and the Friendly Fairies

Once the sun had gone down and the stars were shining brightly, Comet came back into the room. "Come, the telescope is ready," he said. "There is a nice, bright, full moon tonight. Let's go and see it!"

Felix ran excitedly to the telescope and had a look through it. "It's there!" he cried. "My banner is on the moon! Kip, come and have a look!"

As Kip looked through the telescope, he could not help but smile. True enough, Felix's banner was there on the moon, with the message clear enough for all to see.

Only, it wasn't Felix's banner at all, but Kip's copy of it. And it was not actually on the moon – it was just pasted on the lens of the astronomer's telescope!

"This is amazing," said Kip. "The Friendly Fairies will certainly have seen your message. Let's go home and see how your mother is doing!"

Felix, Kip and Comet rushed back to Felix's home. To Kip's surprise, the village doctor was there, examining Felix's mother.

"Hello, Felix! The Friendly Fairies sent me here to look after your mother!" said the village doctor, winking discreetly at Kip and Comet when Felix wasn't looking. "I'll have your mother in good health within a few weeks. Don't you worry!"

Felix was overjoyed. "Mother, you're going to be all right!" he said, tears of joy streaming down his face. "I told you the Friendly Fairies were real!"

Comet and Kip smiled at each other. You see, what Felix didn't know was that it was Comet who had called the doctor and generously paid for the medicine that Felix's mother needed.

So, in a way, Felix was right. The Friendly Fairies were real, but they weren't very far away at all. They were a helpful little pixie called Kip and a kindly old astronomer called Comet!

Run, Richard, Run

Richard was a magnificent golden cockerel. He had a crimson red comb on the top of his head that wobbled as he walked, and his feathers were the colour of warm honey. But he was most proud of his tail. With shining black feathers that curved like a curious question mark, Richard's tail was glorious.

He lived with twelve lady hens in a large outdoor run surrounded by a wire fence. During the day, he was free to wander around and eat as much grass and corn as he could manage. At night, the farmer made sure all the birds were safely tucked up inside the warm wooden coop, away from Mr Fox.

Richard was never lonely. But he was sad, because Richard, unlike all other cockerels, could not crow. Every morning, as the first rays of light trickled into the coop, Richard would stand up and throw his head back. But

Run, Richard, Run

instead of a wonderful ear-blasting "Cock-a-doodle-doo!" Richard could only manage a high-pitched squeak.

One day Melanie the hen was making the others laugh. "When Richard crows, it sounds like he's swallowed a whistle," she said. "He wouldn't even wake an ant up in the morning, let alone frighten the fox." And the whole coop rocked to the sound of giggling hens.

"How can you be so rude?" said Richard, flapping his wings. "I'm the most beautiful cockerel in the world. My tail feathers have won prizes, you know."

"We don't care about your stupid tail," said Melanie. "Your tail won't protect us from Mr Fox."

Later that day, Richard was scratching around in the dry mud on the edge of the pen. His tail feathers drooped as he saw Melanie waddling up to him.

"Richard," she said. "Why aren't you practising your crow? What happens if the fox comes in the middle of the night? You're supposed to warn us."

Richard sighed. "I'm trying. I practise all

the time."

Melanie folded her wings across her chest. "Let's hear it then. Come on, girls, gather round. Richard is going to crow." The other hens bustled over.

"Well... I... um..." Richard stuttered, blushing underneath his golden feathers. Twelve pairs of beady eyes stared. "You see... the thing is..."

"Get on with it!" squawked Melanie unkindly. "We haven't got all day."

Richard took a deep breath so that his chest puffed up like a pillow.

"Cuuuuugh!" he squeaked. "Cuuuuugh!" He tried so hard, his eyes nearly popped out! But it was no good. The only sound he could make was a thin, squeaking whistle.

The hens were almost rolling around on the ground laughing. "Oh dear," Melanie wiped her eyes. "Not very scary, are you, Richard? I don't think Mr Fox will be bothered by your noise."

"Stop it!" said Richard. "You shouldn't speak to me like that."

But the hens stamped and flapped, and their

beaks were wide with laughter. After a while, the laughing died down and Melanie hopped onto the water feeder. "But enough of all this giggling. This is serious. We need our cockerel to be loud and proud." She paused and pointed her wing at the gaggle of hens. "If you don't start crowing properly, soon, we might get a visit from Mr Fox and we don't want to end up as his lunch."

Richard flapped up and down. "We don't need to worry about any foxes. The farmer locks us in at night."

"We can't rely on humans," said Melanie. "What if they forget? What if the door falls off in the middle of the night?"

"She won't forget. She never has before and the door's not going to fall off, is it? That's just silly."

But Melanie wasn't listening. "It's time we did something," she said, holding her wings out wide and nearly toppling off the water feeder.

"Ladies, ladies. I need you all to think. Give me some ideas."

A small hen with moulting feathers shuffled forwards. "My Great Aunt Doris used to say that if you give a cockerel squashed worms it will crow as loud as a lion, and scare even the most ferocious fox away."

"Squashed worms?" said Richard. "How disgusting. I don't even like worms, let alone ones that have been squashed!"

The moulting hen carried on. "They have to be crushed. It makes them into a soothing sludge which goes down your throat and soothes your voice."

Richard stared at her in horror. "Well, I'm

not eating crushed worms."

"Sounds good to me," said Melanie, ignoring his protests. She pointed at four hens. "Girls. Find as many worms as you can and stamp on them. Off you go. Get crushing now. Right away." She turned back to the crowd of hens. "Any more suggestions?"

An even smaller hen spoke next. "My granny told me you have to pour water on mud to make it really wet and sludgy, and then you smooth it all over the cockerel's throat. She told me it seeps through the feathers and makes the cockerel so loud, it shakes the chicken run."

"Watery mud?" Richard dug his claws in the ground. "I will not stand here and be smothered in damp earth. I am a fine, proud cockerel and I deserve a little respect around here."

"Great," Melanie waved at four more chickens. "Sounds like a perfect idea. Tip the water onto the ground, girls. Make us some mud. Any more suggestions?"

Richard sighed and turned his back on the hens. "It's not fair," he thought. "I shouldn't have to put up with this. Why can't I crow like a proper cockerel? Why?"

"Do I have to eat any more?" moaned poor Richard, as the hens told him to eat another squashed worm. "I don't really like worms. I'd much prefer grain or fresh grass and perhaps an ant or two."

"Eat it and stop moaning," said Melanie. The four hens had been jumping on the worms for about an hour. Richard swallowed the last mushy one and felt a bit sick. But maybe it would be worth it. If he could just crow properly, everyone would love him and stop laughing at him all the time.

"Here we go then... are you ready, Melanie? Block your ears, it might hurt." He cleared his throat. "Eeeeeee!" The first noise was not even as loud as the usual squeak. Richard tried again. "Eeeeeeeee!"

Melanie stared. "Well, that's worse than before. Eat another worm!"

"No! I won't! It's not working. It's a silly idea!" He tried to stomp off, but six more hens surrounded him while another one plastered layers of sticky mud onto his throat.

"Oh, my beautiful feathers," gasped Richard.

The mud was cold and smelly and Richard wasn't happy. "I'll show them," he thought. "I'll crow like the fiercest, most vicious eagle of the mountains. I'll be so loud, they'll lose all their feathers and be as bald as eggs." He shook himself free from the hens and threw his head back.

"Eeeeeeeeeee!" he squeaked. "Eeeeeeeee! Oh, ruffle my feathers! It's no good. This mud hasn't helped at all, and neither have those worms. Yuck!"

The hens started laughing again and Richard stamped off to the far corner of the run. "Horrible mud," he muttered. "I feel like a wet mole. I need some nice grass to get rid of the taste of those worms."

To Richard's relief, the hens hadn't followed him and he could at last enjoy some peace.

Pecking at the delicious grass, Richard didn't notice a shadow creeping over the sky. It was only after he'd swallowed a whole beak full of grass that he saw that the sun was going down.

"It's getting dark," he said. "I'll hop into the coop in a minute. This grass is so tasty." As he chomped, Richard could see the girls on the other side of the run gathering at the opening of the coop. "Hurry up, Richard. It's time for bed!" shouted Melanie. "What are you doing over there?"

"Just having a bit more grass," he said. "I'll be there in the shake of a feather."

"Oh, will you now?"

The voice was so low it made Richard's feathers stand on end. He jerked his head up and found himself staring at two sly brown eyes. He gulped.

No! It couldn't be!

Richard was looking at a long nose. Orangey brown, and furry.

Furry?

A fox! It was a fox in their garden! There were its killer teeth, pointed ears and thick black whiskers. It was staring through the wire of the fence!

Richard was so scared he couldn't move. Behind him he could hear the hens filing into the coop and by the calm, sleepy sound of their

clucking, he could tell that they hadn't seen or heard the fox.

"You look rather tasty, I must say," said the fox. He was sitting in the shadow of the trees, his bushy tail sweeping over the ground, lifting up dead leaves. "I think you'd make a great evening snack."

"Run, Richard!" he thought. "Run!" But his feet wouldn't work. It was like he was glued to the ground.

"Why aren't you making that stupid chicken noise?" asked the fox. "That's half the fun, hearing you all squawk."

Still Richard couldn't move. He was frozen with fear. The fox leant closer to the fence, so that his nose pushed right through the wire holes. Richard could see the nostrils moving.

"Mmmm," said the fox, and with one elegant jump he leapt onto the fence, the wire bending under his weight.

At last Richard moved. Clawing at the ground, he turned and stumbled frantically across the chicken run, terror charging up his tail feathers. The fox landed behind him and Richard could feel his the warm breath.

By now the hens had seen the fox and a deafening shriek filled the evening. The whole coop wobbled as they squawked and shoved, trying to jump over each other and get through the gap. "Where's the farmer?" shouted Melanie, her eyes wide in shock. "Why hasn't he shut us in yet? Run, Richard, Run!"

Richard was running as fast as his short legs could carry him, but it was no use. With one giant clash of teeth, the fox reached out and grabbed Richard's tail.

There was a loud ripping sound. Richard gasped.

"My tail," he thought. "My beautiful, amazing, wonderful tail!"

And suddenly Richard wasn't scared. How

dare this furry fool bite his tail? How dare he? He stopped running. Just like that.

Thud.

The fox fell on his nose and went into a sort of forward roll.

"Oof!" said the fox. "Why did you stop?"

"My tail!" said Richard. "You've bitten my bottom!"

It was all too much: the girls laughing at him, the soggy worms, the wet mud and now this. This evil monster, barging into their house and helping himself to Richard's pride and joy.

The chicken run had fallen silent. Twelve hens stared, their eyes like shiny buttons in the early evening gloom.

The fox gazed at Richard, his long nose twitching, tail flicking from side to side. Feathers hung from his mouth.

Slowly, Richard tipped his head back and took a deep breath. His chest puffed up. His claws clamped the ground. The hens held their breaths.

Richard crowed. "Coooooooo!" he squeaked. The fox's eyes widened. His whiskers crinkled. His ears flattened. It was one of Richard's squeakiest crows ever. It peeled through the air and pierced clouds. Mice ran into their burrows. Rabbits scampered out of sight. The trees trembled. And the fox?

The fox cringed. His shoulders came up to his ears and he lolled sideways. "Nooo!" whispered the fox. "I can't stand it. Please stop. Stop that noise." He put his head under his paws and lay on the ground. Richard carried on squeaking.

"Ooh, it hurts," whimpered the fox. "Your crow hurts my ears." He crawled backwards on his tummy. "No more," he said. "Please stop." Richard crowed again, and the fox yelped and slithered back over the fence. Then he disappeared into the trees like a bushy-tailed ghost.

Richard's heart thumped in his chest. He turned round and saw Melanie at the door to the coop. Her beak hung as wide as a drawbridge. For once, she didn't seem to be able to speak.

The farmer's surprised voice made them all jump. "What's going on down here? Sorry

Run, Richard, Run

I'm late, my lovelies. The traffic was so bad I couldn't get home in time." She opened the gate into the pen. "Richard? What are you doing still out?"

On wobbling legs, Richard staggered into the warm coop and hopped on the perch. "Night, everyone," said the farmer. "See you all in the morning."

There was a strange silence inside the hen coop. Everyone seemed to be shaking, but none quite as much as Richard. "What happened out there?" he whispered.

Melanie was still too shaky to sit on her perch. "Your crow hurt the fox's ears. He ran away as soon as you screamed."

"He did, didn't he? It's amazing! I thought my crow was so quiet."

"Yes," said Melanie. "But somehow it got louder when you were scared and angry. And maybe foxes hear things in a different way to us."

"I can't believe it!"

"You're a hero, Richard," said Melanie. "You saved us all."

"Well... I..." Richard could feel himself

turning pink. "I wouldn't call myself a hero."

"It's true," said Melanie, and all the other hens cheered, jumping up and down on the perch, making it wobble.

"Richard saved us!" they shouted. "Richard! Our hero!"

Richard puffed his chest out and felt very proud. He snuggled down on his favourite perch. He was very tired. His bottom felt a bit sore where the feathers had been pulled out, but he still had a few left and they'd soon grow back again. Who needed tail feathers anyway? Not when you had a voice as special and powerful as his, a voice that could melt a fox's eardrums and send him snivelling into the darkness.

Richard smiled to himself as the hens drifted to sleep around him. "I'm a hero," he thought. "I can protect the girls and I don't even have to march up and down showing my tail off. Thank goodness for my special squawk."

And no one ever laughed at Richard again.

The Aliens
Have Landed

"Please, Dad, please can I camp in the
garden?" begged Jonathan as he hopped
around the kitchen in excitement. "We
promise we'll stay in the garden, and David's
mum has said she'll keep her window open so
that she can hear us if we need anything."

"I'll have to think about it," said his dad as
he put the last of the dinner plates into the
cupboard. "We'll see what your mum says
when she comes home."

Jonathan hoped Mum would say yes. It
was August, and very hot outside, and the
long school holidays had become rather
boring. Jonathan always loved going to his
friend David's house, and now David's big
brother Thomas had a new tent and they were
planning to camp out in the garden. David's
mother had agreed, and David had asked if
Jonathan could come too. Jonathan had never

spent a night away from his mum and dad, but he was ready for an adventure. And it would be completely safe after all! David's parents would only be a few metres away in their house, with the bedroom window open.

When Mum came home later that day, Jonathan pleaded again, and promised her that he would tidy the garden shed and his bedroom as a thank-you if she said yes. Mum thought that was a good bargain and so she went to phone David's mother. Jonathan listened at the living-room door. He heard Mum laughing and saying she would be surprised if her son would stay outside all night. This made Jonathan even more determined to have an adventure and prove his mother wrong!

The following day was very busy for Jonathan. He had to help Mum find his sleeping bag, which had been buried under all the winter quilts in the cupboard at the top of the stairs. Next he had to find clean pyjamas, a towel, soap, his toothbrush and a pillow. Then he had to help Mum pack a food box with enough sandwiches, fruit, cake and squash to share with David and Thomas. Last of all he put old battered One Ear Ted on top of the pile. Even though he was old enough to camp without Mum and Dad, he still preferred to have the company of his old faithful friend.

At seven o'clock Mum walked with Jonathan, who was carrying all of his camping kit, down the lane to David's house. Both boys lived in cottages on a twisty lane in the country. The lane was halfway up a hillside so, from their tent, the boys would be able to see for miles. When Jonathan arrived at David's house and saw the tent, high up in the garden, his tummy lurched a little with nervousness. What if he felt scared in the night?

David's parents were sitting in the garden enjoying a cup of tea, and they waved hello.

Mum ruffled the curls on the top of Jonathan's head, and gave him a kiss goodbye. He really wanted to give her a hug. Instead he decided to be brave. He said "Bye!" and quickly disappeared off towards the tent.

Inside the green tent it was very hot and quite dark. David and Thomas were already in there, and greeted him with big grins on their faces. Jonathan laid his sleeping bag down alongside David's and plumped up his pillow on the top – just like Mum did every morning. All the food was outside in a plastic cool box and so they went outside and tucked into ham sandwiches, chunks of cheese and pieces of cake until they were full. It was too early to think about going to sleep – it was still much too light as the sun hadn't started to go down at all. So they decided to play games, read comics and tell scary stories.

Jonathan was not too happy about this but he wouldn't admit it. David told a scary story that Jonathan had heard before and Thomas told one about a haunted house that wasn't really very scary at all. This made Jonathan feel better. Jonathan was just about to begin his own story, which he wasn't looking forward to doing, when David's dad, Mr Taylor, came up to see if they needed anything.

"I'll make sure the tent is properly zipped up on the outside and you must promise to stay inside, to be quiet and to get a good night's sleep," he said. "As the eldest, you're in charge, Thomas. Mum and I are trusting you."

"No need to worry, Dad. I'll make sure

these two behave," he said, grinning at his two friends. David shot out a foot and kicked him on the ankle.

"Now you can tell us your story," said Thomas, once his father had returned to the house. So Jonathan had to tell the only scary story he could think of, which was one he had read in an old book he'd found at Grandma's house. It was all about a crumbling cottage on the edge of the moor and strange noises that came from it at night. A shadow of a man was seen to ride a black horse on winter's nights. David and Thomas listened in silence and Jonathan thought he'd managed to scare them as well as himself!

Soon it was so dark inside the tent that Thomas lit the big torch.

"Hey, can you pull a face like this?" said David, grabbing the torch and putting it under his chin. He pulled such a terrible face that Jonathan batted him over the head with the pillow. All three boys roared with laughter. David handed the torch to Thomas. Thomas's face was even scarier than David's and Jonathan twisted his so much it almost hurt!

This was the funniest game they had ever played and it went on until all three boys lay back on their pillows giggling. By this time the sun had gone down and the tent was a gloomy, purplish colour. In spite of what his father had told him to do, Thomas unzipped the tent.

"I need some fresh air," he said and snaked his way through the opening. Jonathan and David soon joined him and were pleased to see that all the curtains in the house had been drawn. Somehow this made it all the more exciting and daring. They were on their own now!

"Look!" said David, pointing up at the stars. "Isn't that the Plough?" David loved looking at the stars and knew lots of constellations.

"Yes," said Thomas. Then he pointed at a bright light in the sky. "And that bright star there... is Venus."

"That's not a star, silly," said David. "That's a plane. It's moving!" They found this very funny and they started laughing again, nudging each other to be quiet so that they weren't heard.

"Doesn't it make you wonder," asked

Jonathan, "whether there are planets just like ours up there?"

"There must be, for sure," said Thomas. "Probably loads. Some very different ones too, of course." They started talking about what these could be like.

The lights went out one by one in the house and then the garden was in total darkness.

"Better get some sleep, boys," said Thomas, sounding all grown up. The thought of actually sleeping outdoors, just listening to all the sounds of the night, made the boys eager to curl up in their sleeping bags. It was hot in the bags and yet each one secretly found it comforting to be wrapped up snugly. Outside the owls had started hooting and they heard a fox in the distance. Soon, each boy fell asleep.

David was the first to wake. He felt very thirsty. It was so hot in the tent that there were trickles of sweat running down his forehead. He pulled his pyjama top off and began to fan himself with the sleeve. This woke Jonathan and then Thomas, who complained at the younger boys.

"Get back to sleep, you two," he groaned.

"It's too hot, Tom," said David. "Let's just open the zip a bit."

"You know what Dad said," said Thomas. "And I'm in charge."

"So? You're only two years older than me." David reached out and grabbed the zip, pulling it up. A light breeze wafted into the tent.

"Ah, lovely," said David. "See – it's made all the difference. We're all right as long as we stay in the tent."

"All right. Move up and let me get some air too, then," said Thomas. He pushed himself to the front of the tent and stuck his head out.

"Shall we have a drink?" asked Jonathan. "I'm so thirsty."

"Go on then," said Thomas. "Get the squash out of the cool box."

The boys each had a drink, and David was just fitting the top back onto the box when Jonathan yelped. "Look at that!" he whispered, pointing to the hills in the distance. The boys saw a bright light slowly rising above the hills, illuminating the valley below.

"It's like the sun rising, but it can't be dawn just yet," said Thomas. "And besides,

The Aliens Have Landed

the sun rises in the east, and that's west." All three boys stared in wonder as a strange disc-shaped craft rose, slowly and silently, above the hillside. It was just like pictures they had seen in storybooks – a flying saucer!

"Are we seeing things, or is that real?" said Thomas, his voice just a whisper in the silence.

Both boys nodded. They were too amazed and afraid to find words. The spacecraft, for that was most certainly what it was, hovered in the sky just above the arch of the hill and then it lowered and disappeared.

"It's the aliens," said David. "They've landed. It's got to be an invasion."

"Do you think we're the only ones who know?" asked Jonathan.

"We should tell Dad," said Thomas. All three boys crawled out of the tent and ran at full speed down the garden steps, in through the back door and up the stairs to Mr and Mrs Taylor's bedroom. They burst in and Thomas immediately started yelling at his parents.

"Dad, Mum, wake up! Aliens have landed. We've seen the spaceship!"

Mr Taylor grunted and pushed himself up in the bed. Mrs Taylor mumbled and turned over, saying (whilst still half asleep), "Go back to sleep, Thomas."

The boys told Mr Taylor everything they had seen. He smiled and led them to the window, pulling back the curtains.

"A spaceship? Up in the hills over there?"

"Yes," they all said.

"But there's nothing there," said Mr Taylor. When the three boys looked out of the window, they saw that he was right! They felt so silly!

"You must have all been dreaming. Back to the tent, boys."

"No, Dad," argued Thomas. "We all saw it and we weren't even in our sleeping bags. We were outside the tent."

The Aliens Have Landed

"Oh, you were? After all I said about staying inside! Well, are you going back to the garden or not?" The boys didn't reply. "Okay, you can all sleep in Thomas's room. Two of you sleep in the bottom bunk and Thomas in the top. And don't let me hear you again until morning."

When the boys woke up the next day, they were surprised at how long they had slept. David's mum insisted they should sit down at the table and eat breakfast, but they couldn't wait to tell Jonathan's mum and dad about the spaceship. They ran up the lane to Jonathan's house and into the kitchen where his parents were having coffee with his Uncle Bill.

"Hello, campers!" said Jonathan's dad. "Did you have a good time?"

"Mum! Dad! We saw a spaceship on the hill. We saw it rise up and then we saw it land," Jonathan told them excitedly.

"We really did," said Thomas. "We're not making it up and we didn't dream it."

Jonathan's parents smiled but Uncle David said, "Actually I came over the hills very late last night and I saw what you are talking about. I thought I saw the spaceship too!"

The boys couldn't believe their luck. "They have to believe us now," thought Jonathan.

"Why don't we have some breakfast, and then I'll take you up in my car and we'll see what we can find. After all, there might be little green men from another world roaming on our hills!"

After eating their toast and marmalade, the boys clambered into Uncle Bill's car and he drove up through the hills. When they reached the small car park at the viewing point close to where they'd seen the spacecraft, there were three very large trucks and lots of people were milling around. Some were dressed in very strange costumes. One man was dressed in a silver suit – just like an astronaut! It was when they saw him that they realised what had been going on.

"We did see a spaceship," said Jonathan. "But it wasn't real! It was a film prop!"

"Yes, that's right!" said Uncle Bill. "And I'm going to ask that man over there, with the clipboard, if you can see it up close!"

The man with the clipboard introduced himself as the film's producer, and said he'd

be delighted to show the boys around the film set. The old quarry on top of the hill had been transformed into a dusty planet, with strange jagged 'mountains' that the boys discovered were really made of wood. They walked around one of the mountains and there, in front of them, was their spaceship! It turned out to be much smaller than they expected.

"But it's too small for people to get inside!" Jonathan exclaimed.

"That's right," nodded the producer. "It's an optical illusion – against the hillside, in the dark, it looks much bigger than it is."

The boys were fascinated by how the film was shot and when they realised that they could see it take off again they got very excited. The spaceship was attached to long metal poles, like spindly legs, to make it rise up above the hill. When the cameras starting rolling again, the ship rose up, rather shakily at first. Then lights came on all around the middle of the craft and began to flash on and off. This made the ship look as though it was spinning around! There were lots of loudspeakers to make a thrumming noise like an engine. After a few minutes the ship sank slowly back to the ground. The boys were amazed!

When the film director heard how the boys had thought it was a real spaceship, he asked if they would like to meet the actors and crew. They even got to talk to the astronaut who had walked past before. It turned out to be one of the most exciting days of their lives!

"Just think," said Thomas. "When we decided to have our first night's camping we had no idea what an adventure it would turn out to be!"

Suzie's Birthday Surprise

Suzie was very excited. Her friend Nicola was holding a party that night! Suzie had bought Nicola the most perfect present: a teddy that was so cute, you just had to cuddle it! She knew Nicola would absolutely love it, and as she walked along with her Mum to Nicola's house, she couldn't wait to get there. She was wearing her best party dress and her new sparkly shoes and was really looking forward to seeing all her friends. She just wished her Mum would walk a bit faster!

Finally they reached Nicola's house.

"Look!" cried Suzie, pointing excitedly to the top of a bouncy castle in the back garden. Suzie loved bouncing!

She ran up Nicola's path and rang the bell. "Happy birthday!" she cried, as Nicola opened the door. "You didn't tell me you were having a bouncy castle!"

Nicola giggled. "Birthdays are all about surprises!" she said. "You don't know what treats we have for the birthday tea yet, either."

"And you don't know what's in your present," laughed Suzie.

"Thank you very much," said Nicola, looking delighted as she took the shiny parcel. "Shall we play on the bouncy castle? You're the first to arrive. We can have it all to ourselves!"

The two girls had great fun bouncing on the inflatable castle together, and stayed on it until all the other guests arrived. When their other friends had given Nicola her gifts, they started playing party games together. Pass the Parcel and Musical Chairs were Suzie's favourites – when they weren't bouncing on the bouncy castle! Afterwards, they had their party tea. There were sausage rolls and sandwiches, fairy cakes, fruit, pies and jellies. And in the middle of it all was a big birthday cake in the shape of a fairy castle.

"My mum made it!" said Nicola proudly. "I helped her. I helped her make everything for the party. It was such fun! Almost as much fun as eating it all."

Suzie smiled. But inside she felt sad. How she would have loved to have had a birthday party, just once. How she would have enjoyed helping her mum make everything. She used to ask for a party each year on her birthday, but her mum had always told her that their house just wasn't big enough.

"What's the matter?" asked Nicola. "Is there something wrong with your sausage roll? I made those..."

"No," said Suzie, putting it down. "It's lovely." A tear rolled down her cheek.

"What's wrong?" asked Nicola, her face full of concern. "You can't cry at my party. Sadness is not allowed!"

"I just feel so bad," said Suzie, sniffing.

"About what?" Nicola asked, putting her arm around her.

"We don't have room at my house for a party, so I can never have one with all of my friends, like you do. And I don't want my mum to feel bad about it. We can't help having a small house. It just makes me sad."

"We all understand," said Nicola. "We don't mind that you can't have a party."

Suzie blinked back a tear. But she did! How she longed to decorate her home with balloons and streamers, and make a party tea and have everyone sing 'Happy Birthday' to her. But it was never going to happen while they lived in their house. She blinked back her tears and forgot about her sadness for a while. They played more games after tea, until finally it was time to go home.

"Did you have a good time?" Suzie's mum asked her as they left.

"Yes, I loved it!" said Suzie, but there

was a tinge of sadness in her voice as she remembered getting upset earlier in the day. She told herself she was being silly, she had had a good time...

Her mum sensed what was wrong. "You know, Suzie, I've got an idea. It's your birthday next month. Why don't we hold a birthday party for you?"

Suzie stared at her in confusion. "But I didn't think we had room at home."

"We don't, not in the house, but the garden is bigger. So I thought we could have it outside!" her mum replied. "How about we hire a marquee?"

"What's that?" Suzie asked curiously.

"It's like a big tent with windows," said her mum. "It goes outside and you can hold a party in it." A tent with windows! How amazing! Suzie thought it sounded brilliant.

"Oh, yes please!" cried Suzie, jumping up and down. "I'd love to have a party! It's going to be great. I know just what games we can play, and what lovely food we can have..." And she listed everything she'd eaten at Nicola's house that day.

"We could have some different food, too," said her mum. "We could bake cookies, and serve them still warm from the oven."

"Oh yes!" cried Suzie, her eyes shining. Even though she'd eaten a lot at Nicola's party, she was starting to feel hungry again!

"Nicola told me birthday parties are all about surprises," she said, excitedly. "How can we give my friends a big surprise? We haven't got room for a bouncy castle in the back garden. Not with a marquee!"

"Why don't we only tell their mummies and daddies about the party," suggested her mum. "We could ask them to keep it a secret and then on the day of the party, they could pretend they are going shopping. Instead, they can bring your friends to our house."

"Oh yes!" Suzie cried. She was so excited she thought she'd burst. "I can't wait to see their faces when they realise they're at my party! What a surprise!"

Suzie could think of nothing else but her party for the next four weeks. She and her mum planned everything from the moment her friends arrived until the minute they left.

Suzie's Birthday Surprise

Her mum knew of lots of games that Suzie had never even heard of, and they practised playing them. There was bobbing for apples, Musical Statues, Guess Who I Am and Pin the Tail on the Donkey. Suzie wrote out all the invitations and posted them in the post box. She blew up all the balloons and helped ice her birthday cake, which was a lovely seaside scene with sugar-paste mermaids, white chocolate dolphins and a beach made of brown sugar!

Finally, it was the day of Suzie's birthday party. It was grey and windy, but Suzie didn't care. "Bring on the rain! Bring on the wind!" she cried, gazing out of the window as the leaves danced around the garden. "We'll be so cosy in the marquee!"

Then there was a knock at the door. "That will be the marquee delivery," her mum said.

But it wasn't. It was the man from the tent company, looking very sad. "I'm so sorry," he said. "But the marquee was torn yesterday and we haven't got a spare replacement in that size. We can't give you one today."

Suzie stared at him, tears filling her eyes. "But you have to!" she said in a wobbly voice.

"I'm sorry," the man said. "There's a huge hole in it. The previous client damaged it quite badly. It won't keep anyone dry."

Suzie turned to her mum. "What are we going to do?" she wailed.

"We'll get one from somebody else," her mum reassured her.

But the tent man shook his head. "I'm sorry," he said. "I've already asked around to try to get one for you. There isn't one to be had anywhere. Not of the size you need."

"Well, we'll just have to have my party in the garden without the tent!" Suzie said bravely. But when she looked outside again, it started to rain. "This is a disaster!"

"No, it isn't!" said her mum. "We'll fit

everyone in... somehow. We'll fold down the table and everyone can sit around on the floor. They can eat off their laps. I'm afraid there won't be room for Musical Statues, though."

Of course there wouldn't! There would be no room to dance around at all. Suzie gazed miserably at the donkey she'd made to pin the tail onto, and the big tub filled with apples for apple bobbing. They wouldn't have room for any of the games she'd planned. And without a table, where would they put the birthday cake so she could blow out her candles?

"We'll sort the house out, Suzie. We've got time before the party starts," said her mum as cheerfully as she could. "The important thing is that all your friends come."

Suzie tried to stay cheerful. She and her mum hurriedly cleared space for everyone and had just about finished their work by three o'clock, when the party was due to start. Suzie ran to the window to look out for her friends, but couldn't see anyone down the street.

Nobody came at five past, or even ten past three. Suzie anxiously hurried outside to look for her friends and to see if anyone was rushing up the road, but there was no sign of anybody. "What's happened?" she cried.

"I don't know," said her mum. "It's a surprise, so you didn't talk about it to any of your friends. So we don't know who can come... or even if the invitations arrived safely. Did you put the right addresses on?"

Suzie's heart sank. She stared at her mum miserably. "I didn't put any addresses!" she said. "I just put 'To Nicola's Mum', 'To Max's Mum', 'To Pippa's Dad' like that, and then put them in the post box."

"Oh dear," said her mum. "I don't think anyone actually got them, then. No one knows about your party."

Suzie couldn't believe it. She was heartbroken. "No one's coming!" she cried. "My first ever party and it's a total disaster. This is the most awful birthday surprise ever!"

"Well, we'll just have to go and fetch them," said her mum, putting on her coat and then putting Suzie's on for her. "Come on!"

Suzie hurriedly followed her mum out. They started at Max's house, but he wasn't in. Neither were Lucy or Tom. Everyone was out! It was another disaster.

"This is useless," said Suzie, as they reached Nicola's house, the last one of all. But even though they thought they heard a noise from inside, no one answered the door. "Oh, please! Surely Nicola wants to see me on my birthday?" groaned Suzie.

"Suzie!" Suzie twirled round. There was Nicola with her mum, and they were rushing up the garden path towards her. "Happy Birthday!" cried Nicola.

"Is it?" asked Suzie, miserably.

"How funny that you're here!" Nicola continued. "We've just been to your house to invite you round to mine."

"But I want you to come to mine," said Suzie sadly.

"Let's go inside while we sort this out," said Nicola's mum, opening the front door. "You go first, Suzie." Suzie stepped inside.

"Surprise!" cried all her friends, leaping out from behind chairs and curtains.

Suzie stood there, stunned. She looked around at all their smiling faces and the birthday balloons and streamers everywhere.

"You told me at my party how much you wanted to have one of your own!" Nicola said. "So I asked everyone to come round here as a surprise birthday party for you. We don't have a birthday tea—"

"Yes we do!" laughed Suzie's mum. "It's round at our house. If everyone would like to come and help fetch it, we can have Suzie's party here. If that's all right, Suzie?"

Suzie smiled. It was brilliant! She would have a birthday party with all of her friends, after all. And at Nicola's house they'd have so much more room to play. It was brilliant!

So, laughing happily, everyone hurried round to Suzie's house to help bring the food over. On the way back Suzie carried her big donkey picture for them to pin the tail onto, and she led a long procession of people carrying cakes, sandwiches, sausages, jellies, cookies and the biggest, most beautiful birthday cake anyone had ever seen.

"Well," said Nicola as they reached her house. "Is this a good birthday surprise?"

"The best ever!" Suzie laughed. What could possibly be better?